"No, Don't," She Gasped.

Heedlessly, he drew her to him, and his insistent lips parted hers. Lindsay knew she should break away, put an end to this madness, but already an intoxicating excitement coursed through her. Never had she craved a man like this, longed for his touch, his love, his body.

Then, as her lips moved against his with unrestrained need, Philip suddenly pulled away.

"You really are full of surprises," he said, his voice thick and barely controlled. "I know what your little game is, but it isn't going to work. Your husband did his best to destroy the vineyard and I'm not going to let you do the same!"

ERIN ROSS

has pursued a wide variety of activities during her life. At one time or another, this author studied radio, taught guitar, practiced karate and sang with a rock group. But writing has always been a favorite pursuit. "I'm an avid reader," she explains, "and I think sooner or later all avid readers get the bug to write!"

Dear Reader:

SILHOUETTE DESIRE is an exciting new line of contemporary romances from Silhouette Books. During the past year, many Silhouette readers have written in telling us what other types of stories they'd like to read from Silhouette, and we've kept these comments and suggestions in mind in developing SILHOUETTE DESIRE.

DESIREs feature all of the elements you like to see in a romance, plus a more sensual, provocative story. So if you want to experience all the excitement, passion and joy of falling in love, then SILHOUETTE DESIRE is for you.

I hope you enjoy this book and all the wonderful stories to come from SILHOUETTE DESIRE. I'd appreciate any thoughts you'd like to share with us on new SILHOUETTE DESIRE, and I invite you to write to us at the address below:

Karen Solem
Editor-in-Chief
Silhouette Books
P.O. Box 769
New York, N.Y. 10019

ERIN ROSS
Second Harvest

Silhouette Desire

Published by Silhouette Books New York

America's Publisher of Contemporary Romance

SILHOUETTE BOOKS, a Simon & Schuster Division of
GULF & WESTERN CORPORATION
1230 Avenue of the Americas, New York, N.Y. 10020

Distributed by Pocket Books

ISBN: 0-671-45227-4

First Silhouette Books printing September, 1982

10 9 8 7 6 5 4 3 2 1

America's Publisher of Contemporary Romance

Printed in the U.S.A.

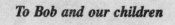

To Bob and our children

Second Harvest

1

Lindsay caught her first sight of Kia Ora from the top of a rolling green hill. To the left, row upon row of vines stretched out for acres under the late afternoon sun, the grapes plump and juicy, nearly ready for harvesting. She could hardly believe that half of these acres had been Alex's. And now, since his death, they were hers, shared with a man that until two weeks ago she had not known existed.

"Kia Ora Vineyard is all that's left of your husband's inheritance," the lawyer, Mr. Bermann, had explained. "It's located in New Zealand's Henderson Valley and has been in the Macek family for four generations, starting with your husband's great-grandfather, Ljuba Macek, who migrated from Yugoslavia in the 1800s. In Maorian tradition, Ljuba called his vineyard *Kia Ora*, which means 'good luck,' and certainly the property has thrived throughout almost a century of Maceks. When Alex's father, Josef Macek, died nine years ago, the vineyard passed to your husband and his cousin, Philip Macek, with the provision that neither partner could sell his share of the vineyard without the other's consent. Josef's will also stipulates that in the event of either cousin's death, the heirs must assume a working interest in the vineyard for a certain period of time or the business reverts wholly to the surviving partner. Specifically," the lawyer had concluded solemnly, "if you do not spend three months on the property, you will lose it."

"But I don't understand," Lindsay had protested, overwhelmed by this discovery. "If Kia Ora is such an important part of the Macek family, why didn't Alex mention it to me?"

Mr. Bermann had cleared his throat uncomfortably, obviously wishing Alex had been more forthright with his wife. "I'm afraid that your husband was, well, somewhat of a disappointment to his father, my dear. When Alex left New Zealand ten years ago it was not under the most amicable of circumstances. Very possibly Kia Ora represented a part of his life he preferred to forget."

Lindsay shivered despite the warm sunshine bathing the Land Rover Philip Macek had dispatched to bring her to Kia Ora. What if the Macek family resented her intrusion—her invasion of their island paradise? Philip Macek's note, formally inviting her to visit Kia Ora, had been succinct, almost to the point of incivility, as if he were discharging an unpleasant duty. Still, she thought, as they reached the western fringe of the vineyard, half of Kia Ora was legally hers, and she had every intention of at least seeing the property before making a final decision.

The Macek house and winery stood close together at the end of a long, tree-lined driveway. The house had three stories with several English-style turrets and chimneys: a charming old place that Lindsay felt sure was the original structure. Rough-hewn stone surrounded the high-arched doorway and continued around most of the first floor. To the left side of the house was a covered porch extending out over a well-tended garden alive with color. Beyond the house loomed the winery, old, but obviously remodeled.

As the driver stopped the Land Rover before the imposing old structure, a stout woman in her early fifties threw open the front door and hurried out to greet them. Just above the woman's head Lindsay saw a movement from an upstairs window, but a quick look caught only a fleeting glimpse of a small pink face before it disappeared behind the curtains. One of the servants, Lindsay wondered? If so, she must be very young, and very shy judging by her quick retreat.

As Lindsay started up the steps leading to the front door she was startled to find a large arm draped around her waist and a round, full face grinning into hers.

"So this is Alex's wife," the woman said cheerfully, her voice deep and earthy. "I'm Inia—Inia Muru, the housekeeper. Mr. Philip's in Auckland for the day on business, but he said to make you comfortable." The woman's strong arm gave Lindsay a quick squeeze, then bent to pick up her two suitcases as if they were feather light. "Let's not stand out here all afternoon. I've got a leg of lamb in the oven that won't do if it's burned black. Besides, Stephie's havin' a fit to see her new cousin."

The moment Lindsay was introduced to Stephanie Macek she knew this was the face she had seen peeking out the window. Pretty and very slender, the little girl could not have been more than nine or ten. Her small face was tan and solemn as she regarded

11

Lindsay shyly through huge dark-blue eyes. Two long black pigtails hung down her back reaching almost to the waist of her well-worn blue jeans. Although the child's eyes never left Lindsay, she didn't say a word, peering out at her instead from behind Inia's broad back.

"What's the matter, Stephie?" the housekeeper chided, taking hold of the little girl's arm. "You come out here and say hello to Miss Lindsay. What's she gonna think of you hidin' back there like you've never been taught better manners?"

"That's all right," Lindsay said, embarrassed for the child. "She'll make friends in her own time."

"It doesn't do any good to spoil her," Inia clucked, but Lindsay noticed that the swat she directed to the little girl's bottom was more affectionate than disciplinary. "You get along, now, and finish peeling those potatoes," the housekeeper told the child, grinning broadly. "Now, if I could just find that lazy girl of mine I'd have her see you to your room. You must be ready to drop. Kiri!" the woman bellowed.

"Right here, Mama," came an airy voice. Lindsay watched as a young, heavily made-up girl of about eighteen came dancing lightly toward them. "I was just seeing to the dusting," she explained, unperturbed by the older woman's dark look.

The housekeeper shook her head so sharply that the wiry cluster of salt-and-pepper curls surrounding her full face bounced from the movement. "I know well and good what you were seeing to," she said. "You were buried up to your nose in those fashion magazines again." Inia smiled resignedly at Lindsay. "This is my daughter, Kiri. She's a good enough girl when her head isn't stuck up in some cloud. Spends too much time readin' those glamour magazines, though. Doesn't do any good dreamin' about things you're never likely to have."

Kiri looked undaunted, as if she and her mother had been through this many times before. "But I do mean to have them, Mama," she said good-naturedly. "I don't intend to spend the rest of my life in Henderson Valley."

"Never mind what you intend to do," Inia told her sharply. "Right now I want you to show Miss Lindsay to her room. And help her unpack, too." She turned toward the kitchen. "I'll see to the roast while you settle in. Dinner should be ready in about an hour. Come on down as soon as you finish."

Kiri led Lindsay up two flights of stairs and then down a passageway to the right. Lindsay suspected she was in the guest wing of the old house since most of the rooms they passed looked unoccupied. Toward the end of the hall, Kiri pushed open a door leading into a lovely bedroom furnished in pale blue and cream. Three of the walls were papered in off white with delicate bouquets of violets held together with tiny pink bows. The fourth wall was painted a soft shade of blue, which brought out the dark, rich hue of the flowers. The bed was large and looked comfortable, the ruffled spread a pretty cream color with several pastel-blue throw pillows scattered about the head. It was a warm, inviting room, and Lindsay felt immediately at home.

"Mr. Philip said you were to have this room," Kiri said, "although I don't know why. The family wing is at the other end of the house. Since you were Mr. Alex's wife, seems like you should be there."

"Never mind, Kiri," Lindsay said, just as glad she wasn't in the same wing as the family. "This is a beautiful room. I'll be very comfortable here."

The next fifteen minutes passed pleasantly as Kiri helped Lindsay unpack. The young girl exclaimed loudly with each new item that came from the suitcase. Lindsay watched Kiri in amusement, wondering what she would say if she knew that the most recent acquisition was two years old. All the clothes dated from a time when she was expected to dress expensively and in the latest fashion, as befitted the wife of a film studio president. It was a credit to her fine sense of cut and fabric that most of the clothes looked as fresh and fashionable now as they had when they were purchased. Lindsay had learned early that a simple, well-cut garment kept its style far longer than the more trendy numbers.

"How long have you and your mother been at Kia Ora?" Lindsay asked, as they hung the clothes neatly in the closet.

"I was born here," Kiri replied brightly, "and Mama's been here since she was about my age. She came to work at Kia Ora when Mr. Philip and Mr. Alex were just little boys."

"Your mother must be a great help to Mrs. Macek," Lindsay said, smoothing the wrinkles out of a knit suit. "She seems very good with Stephanie."

Kiri looked confused. "Mrs. Macek? But there's no Mrs. Macek, except for you, of course. Mr. Philip's never been married. Not that the women around here haven't tried," she added lightly.

It was Lindsay's turn to look startled. "But Stephanie—I mean, what about the child?"

Kiri finished hanging a sweater, then smiled. "Oh, that. Yes, she's Philip's daughter. But he wasn't married to the child's mother." Her voice lowered conspiratorially. "They were engaged, you see, and very much in love. I don't remember too much of it

14

because I was only seven or eight at the time. But Mama tells me it was a real tragedy. When his fiancée found out she was going to have his baby she went away without even telling him. Then, later, when she came back with the child, Philip was very angry and wanted to marry her right away."

"But he didn't."

"No. No one knows why, but they say she acted very strangely. Some said she had a real bad case of baby blues."

"Postpartum depression?"

"Yes, that's it. Anyway, when the baby was about six months old, she took too many sleeping pills one night and never woke up."

"You mean she did it on purpose? She committed suicide?"

The girl shrugged her slim shoulders. "Who knows? Some people said it was because she had the baby like that. But Mama says there was another story going around at the time that Mr. Philip did something awful to her and she never got over it. That stood Mama's hair on end, I can tell you. She says Mr. Philip tried to do the right thing and that he would never have hurt her deliberately."

Lindsay nodded, but the surprising story left her wondering even more about the enigmatic Philip Macek. True, he had acknowledged the child as his daughter and raised her in his home, but under the circumstances it was the least he could do. What was Philip Macek really like? And what had he done to drive that poor woman to such a desperate act? Lindsay felt a momentary twinge of anxiety. Who was this man whose life was now so intricately entangled with hers?

Suddenly, Lindsay felt guilty for encouraging Kiri to

discuss her employer's private life. "You said down-stairs that you planned to leave Henderson," she said, changing the subject. "Where will you go?"

"Oh, probably to Australia. Maybe even the United States. You see, I'm going to be a model, and the opportunities aren't very good in New Zealand."

"And I take it your mother doesn't think much of your plans."

The girl made a face. "Mama worries too much. And she's got this thing about preserving the Maori tradition. She wants me to settle down and marry a nice Maori boy and have lots of babies."

"Does she have anyone in mind?"

Lindsay was surprised to see Kiri blush slightly under her golden brown complexion.

"She wants me to marry Michael Taira. He works here on the vineyard."

"And you don't like her choice?"

"Oh, Michael's all right," Kiri admitted. "But he's almost twenty-one, and he'll never go any further than this vineyard. He has no future. I want something better than Mama's had."

"But your mother looks very happy," Lindsay pointed out.

"Maybe. But she hasn't known anything else. I know there's a better life outside of this island, and I mean to have it."

After the girl left, Lindsay showered, then towel dried her long, golden blond hair as she stood looking out the window at endless rows of Kia Ora vines. Again she thought of her late husband and the startling series of events which had led her to the vineyard. She could still picture Alex's handsome face, his eyes daring and alive, his curly blond hair rakishly askew. Perhaps it had been his very impulsiveness, the irrepressible buoyancy of his nature which had lured her away from the security of a rural Iowa farming town and into the fast lane of Alex's Hollywood. Certainly, in the six years of their marriage, she had never suspected a more provincial side to her husband's past. It was as if nothing had existed for Alex before Cinetelle Productions became his one driving obsession, a passkey into the tinseled world of glamour and self-gratification.

Well, Alex had enjoyed, all right, Lindsay thought ruefully, his dalliances made easy by the swarms of beautiful young starlets eager to land that first big part. Finally, in the fourth year of their marriage, Lindsay had left, using what remained of her savings to return to school and earn a secondary teaching degree in dramatics. After that she heard little about Alex except for an occasional review extolling, or more often panning, this or that film. Cinetelle's last two years must have been disastrous to have wiped out Alex's sizable inheritance. Then, last week, had come the shocking, the unbelievable, news. Alex Macek's life had been snuffed out, taken from him in a freak accident on location in the Bahamas, leaving her a widow at twenty-five.

Lindsay sighed as she watched the sun set behind the long rows of grapes, her large brown eyes reflecting glittering highlights from the fleeting rays as it descended. Kia Ora was all that was left of Alex's turbulent past. And as she watched the final strokes of brilliant color fade from the New Zealand skyline, she wondered what part the vineyard would play in her future.

When Lindsay came down to dinner half an hour later she found just Stephanie waiting at the table. Mr.

Philip was still not back, Inia explained, adding that long hours were not unusual at this time of year when everything was being readied for the harvest.

"And, of course, there's so much at stake this year because of the varietals," she added matter-of-factly.

"Varietals?" Lindsay repeated, frustrated by her lack of knowledge concerning the vineyard.

"That's a wine made from a certain variety of grape, or at least *mostly* from one kind of grape. Mr. Philip has been aging some Cabernet Sauvignon for nearly four years now. Real tricky it is, too."

Lindsay's curiosity was piqued. "And this wine is particularly important to Kia Ora?"

Inia beamed with pride. "So far New Zealand has never had a really great wine, something to make the Henderson Valley famous. But Mr. Philip's gonna change all that when he finally opens his varietals this year."

"It sounds like an ambitious project."

"And expensive," the housekeeper said, putting several overflowing dishes onto the table. "I overheard Mr. Philip say the investment in new vines alone was tremendous, and then he had to wait a good five years for them to mature enough to bear grapes. And that's not to mention all the modernization he had to do. He's even ordered a mechanical harvester this year to help take care of the increased crop. And, of course, there's Mr. Hansen, the fellow in Auckland who's testin' our grapes all the time."

"You mean an enologist?" Lindsay volunteered, pleased to know something about the subject.

"That's him. Anyway, a lot depends on the success of those grapes."

"And if he fails—"

Inia shook her wiry head. "Then Mr. Philip will have to sell Kia Ora. Already he's had offers for the vineyard; very generous offers. And there's some that think he's crazy not to get out—now, before the harvest."

"But he'd prefer to take the risk that the varietals will succeed?"

"Mr. Philip isn't afraid of taking risks," Inia said simply. "But he won't fail. He knows his business. The vineyard's in his blood."

The housekeeper wiped her hands on a crisp, starched apron and brusquely motioned Lindsay to the table. "That's enough of that kind of talk. Dinner's not gonna be any better if it's cold." She pulled out a chair. "Here, you sit down across from Stephie. And eat hearty. I've made a special dinner for your first night at Kia Ora."

But despite Inia's attempts at a festive meal, dinner was a lonely affair. Repeatedly, Lindsay attempted to draw Stephanie into conversation, but the timid child merely retreated farther into her shell. Fortunately, the food was excellent. For all Inia's worries about the lamb, it was done to perfection, slightly pink and juicy, and very tender. The vegetables, Stephanie's proud contribution to the meal, were suitably praised by Lindsay, as was the steaming hot bread, one of Inia's specialties. Dessert was especially good, *Pavlova*, meringue with sliced fruit and whipped cream, which Inia told her was traditional fare in New Zealand. Still, Lindsay ate sparingly, unable to shake the vague apprehension which had gripped her since her arrival at Kia Ora. It was a relief when Inia at last gave up trying to refill her plate and shooed them out of the dining room to have coffee and hot chocolate in the den.

There, despite the cozy atmosphere, the silence of the old house seemed to close about them, increasing Lindsay's anxiety. She found herself jumping at every sound, each creak and footstep which echoed through the dwelling. What's the matter with me? she asked herself in annoyance. Surely her frayed nerves couldn't be due to Philip Macek's overdue appearance. Why should the thought of meeting Alex's cousin fill her with such foreboding?

Finally, to break the silence, Lindsay tried to draw Stephanie into a conversation. But to each question she asked about school, friends or hobbies, the little girl merely replied with a polite yes or no, contributing nothing else to the exchange. Eventually, Lindsay pieced together the information that there were few children Stephanie's age near Kia Ora and that the little girl was too shy to make many friends at school. The child badly needs to be pulled out of her shell, she thought, and her heart went out to the timid little girl. If only Stephanie would accept her as a friend. There must be some way to give her more self-confidence.

"How was your dinner, Peanut?" came a low voice, startling Lindsay out of her thoughts.

Looking up, Lindsay saw a tall, powerfully built man standing just inside the door. He was wearing work clothes: tight fitting jeans, heavy boots and a plaid, short-sleeved shirt open low on the chest to reveal a thatch of curly black hair.

Stephanie looked shyly at Lindsay before answering. "My vegetables were good, Papa. Inia says I may try making the dessert tomorrow."

"That's great, Peanut," Philip said, walking over and planting a kiss on the child's forehead. "But now I want you to get yourself upstairs. It's past your bedtime."

Lindsay watched the child disappear up the stairs, then felt Philip Macek's eyes on her and was amazed to find her pulse racing under his scrutiny.

"I presume your room is satisfactory?" he asked.

"It's very nice, thank you," Lindsay answered, matching his formality.

"There's no need to thank me," he told her abruptly. "You're half owner, remember?"

"Yes, I'd almost forgotten. It takes some getting used to."

"It will take a great deal of getting used to," he agreed, and Lindsay sensed resentment behind the words. Philip's eyes continued to bore into hers, their unflinching intensity seeming to strip even her soul bare for his inspection.

Feeling suddenly, and maddeningly, self-conscious under his examination, Lindsay reached for a cup from the table.

"Coffee?" she asked, and was surprised that her voice sounded off its normal timbre.

"No, thank you," Philip answered. He moved to the well-stocked wet bar at the end of the room. "I prefer something stronger."

Lindsay watched as he poured himself a whiskey, and for the first time she was aware of his resemblance to Alex. Perhaps she had failed to notice it immediately because of the much more conspicuous difference in their personalities. Where Alex had been a compulsive extrovert, basking in public attention, his cousin seemed supremely sure of his own importance, with no need for ego-boosting from the outside world. And certainly there was nothing similar in their coloring: Alex's fair skin and hair were in sharp contrast to Philip's dark, almost rugged good looks. What was it, then, in this overbearing man that reminded her of Alex? She realized it was the same determined set of the mouth and the slightly hooked aquiline nose that both men shared, and the familiar indentation in the strong chin. But the eyes, no, there was no likeness there. Where Alex's pale blue eyes had changed with the impulsiveness of his moods, Philip's, of the most amazing cobalt, gave the illusion of impregnable depths. She already knew they could probe hers with a compelling, nerve-wracking intensity.

"How much did Alex tell you about Kia Ora?" Philip said at last, turning to lean his broad back against the bar.

"Not much," Lindsay answered. Then, more honestly, "In fact, nothing at all."

Philip gave a short laugh in which there was no humor. "I'm not surprised. I always had the impression that Kia Ora was more like a prison to Alex than a home. It almost broke his father's heart when his only son left New Zealand ten years ago without so much as a goodbye."

Lindsay hardly knew what to say, so blatant was the hostility in Philip Macek's voice.

"I had no idea—"

"I'm sure you didn't," Philip said in a clipped tone. "Why should you have cared about an old man and his dreams? Alex certainly didn't."

"But I'm sure if Alex had known—"

"You think that would have made a difference?" Philip Macek moved to stand directly in front of Lindsay's chair, and, from her low viewpoint, he seemed to loom taller than his six feet two or three inches. Not for the first time since Alex's cousin entered the den, Lindsay felt herself at a disadvantage.

"Since it appears you will be staying here—for a time, at least," he said, underscoring his words carefully, "I think you should know exactly what you've gotten yourself into."

As Philip paused, Lindsay could hear a grandfather clock strike the hour from another part of the house, emphasizing the charged silence in the den. Her eyes seemed drawn to the imposing man before her.

"My cousin and I did not get along," Philip continued. "We never did get along, even as boys. Alex had no use for the land. He was always restless, always looking for excitement and power, even if it was at the expense of others."

"Alex was creative," Lindsay objected, feeling a guilty need to champion her husband's memory. "He needed an outlet for his energies."

"Yes, well, he found it, didn't he?" Philip's eyes moved slowly and appraisingly over every inch of her slim figure, causing an embarrassing warmth to color her cheeks, a flush that, unknown to Lindsay, contrasted strikingly with her fair complexion and long, honey-blond hair. "Alex always did have good taste. Still, I'm surprised you managed to catch him. The cream of Henderson Valley tried and failed before you."

"Manipulation is hardly necessary when two people are in love," Lindsay replied hotly.

Philip's eyes were mocking. "And you were?"

"Yes, Mr. Macek, we were. Not that it's any of your business. Alex and I were very much in love." Or at least I was, Lindsay thought, shaken by the grain of truth in Philip's words.

"Then that's the first time Alex ever cared for anyone other than himself. I wouldn't have thought it possible." His eyes raked over her one more time. "How fortunate that Alex was able to find such a beautiful woman to help him spend his father's money." His blue eyes rested on hers accusingly, as if she had been an accessory to her husband's irresponsible behavior. Bright spots of anger flared on Lindsay's cheeks. But of course, she remembered, holding her temper in check, he doesn't know we were separated. Well, let him think what he wants. She wouldn't give him the satisfaction of a denial.

"And now you've come to Kia Ora to claim your inheritance," Philip went on.

"I've come to examine Alex's holdings, yes," Lindsay answered evenly, fighting to keep the rising anger out of her voice. "I think I owe him that, at least."

"As well as yourself," he added, with biting sarcasm. "Kia Ora is a very valuable piece of property, Mrs. Macek. If it hadn't been for the provisions in my uncle's will, I'm sure it would have been squandered along with the rest of Alex's inheritance." His eyes mocked her smooth, white hands and elegantly shod feet. "Now I'm afraid you're going to have to work for your share."

"I assure you I'm not afraid of a little work, Mr. Macek," Lindsay clipped.

Philip's eyebrows rose questioningly. "Oh? I'm glad to detect such enthusiasm. You're going to need it."

Maddeningly, he turned his back on her and moved to the bar, as if the conversation was of no more interest to him, and Lindsay had the infuriating impression of being dismissed.

"If you're interested, I'll give you a tour of the vineyard tomorrow morning," he added as an afterthought. He looked her over appraisingly. "That is, if you have something more suitable to wear than that outfit."

Lindsay looked down at the elegantly cut beige silk dress Kiri had helped her select for dinner. Left on her own, she would have picked something simpler, but eager to make friends with the girl, Lindsay had reluctantly given in to Kiri's choice. Now she could see she must look indolent and spoiled in Philip's eyes.

Lindsay shifted in her seat, as if by doing so she could cover up the offending dress. "Of course I'm interested," she said stiffly. "That's why I came to Kia

Ora, remember? And don't worry. I'll be dressed appropriately. I plan to pull my own weight."

Philip eyed her doubtfully. "That remains to be seen." He drained his drink and set it on the counter. "I'll expect you downstairs at six o'clock sharp tomorrow morning. Think you can handle that?"

He smiled at her, but she saw only his mocking, dark blue eyes. "We'll see tomorrow what kind of a *vigneron* you make."

2

~eeeeeeeeee~

Lindsay was up before dawn the next morning. She slipped into a pair of blue denim pants and a soft cotton shirt, then carefully drew her fine blond hair into a ponytail at the crown of her head. Pulling on a pair of well-worn tennis shoes, she hurried downstairs for a quick cup of coffee before her tour of the vineyard. It was somewhat deflating to hear that Philip had eaten over an hour ago and was already at work.

"He said he'd be back to get you at six," Inia explained, piling steaming red snapper and eggs onto her plate. In the center of the table she set down a plate of hot bread and a mound of sweet butter.

Lindsay looked at her heaped plate in dismay. "Inia, I'm sorry, but I can't possibly eat all this. It looks wonderful, but—"

"Nonsense," the woman scolded, "you're in the

country now. You need more than coffee in the morning or you'll never get through the day. Now, you just lay a fork into that fish. It'll melt in your mouth."

Doubtfully, Lindsay did as she was told and was amazed by the delicately succulent taste of the fresh snapper. "This is delicious," she raved, eating more without being coaxed.

Inia beamed. "Good. Now you sound more like a Macek. Soon as you finish up I'll bring you some fresh fruit."

Laughing, Lindsay protested, but was surprised to find herself enjoying the sweet tang of the Chinese gooseberry, or kiwi fruit, which Inia presented to end the meal. She was sipping her coffee when Philip returned.

"So you made it up in time," he said, accepting a cup of coffee from Inia. His gaze took in her outfit, resting for just a moment on her slim waist and the gentle swell of her young breasts straining beneath the shirt. But if she thought he would compliment her on her choice of clothing she was disappointed. Gulping down the last of his coffee he rose from his chair.

"It's getting late. Let's get on with it."

Swallowing a sharp retort, Lindsay followed him outside into the cool morning sunshine.

"Let's start out there, in the fields," he said, climbing into a pickup truck parked behind the house.

They bumped along the dirt roads outlining the long rows of vines until they came to the crest of a hill, where Philip stopped. From this vantage point the gentle landscape spread out for miles around them, affording a panoramic view of the property. Lindsay held her breath as she looked out over the fertile acres, so reminiscent of the bountiful fields of her birth. She had been here less than twenty-four hours and already she was in love with the countryside.

"It's beautiful," she said softly.

"Yes. It's also risky, temperamental and a hell of a lot of backbreaking work." He swept his muscular arm around in an arch. "In late winter these canes are so barren they almost look dead. Then, in early spring the limbs develop little patches of leaves that will later bear the grapes. That's when the worry starts. One night of spring frost can cut the harvest by ten percent. A month of frost can wipe out the whole vineyard."

"But isn't there something you can do?"

"Not much. Naturally, we use heaters and blowers, but we can only cut our losses, not eliminate them." Philip walked over to the nearest vines and motioned Lindsay to look under the leaves. "Do you see the wires in there? Every year hundreds of vines have to be stapled with trellis wires to direct their growth. Then sucker canes have to be removed from each plant or they'll sap the vines of energy. Sometimes we have to thin the foliage to let more sun get through to the fruit. Then we spray two or three applications of sulfur to guard against mildew."

"It sounds like a lot of work."

"It is. And a little bit of luck doesn't hurt. Our harvest will begin in a couple of weeks, which means a lot of preparation now. All the harvesting gear has to be washed and the fermenting tanks scoured, and the tanks that will hold the new wine have to be sterilized with sulfur. The men call it our autumn housecleaning." He looked at her speculatively. "Not quite like ordering the maid to vacuum the carpet and turn out the beds, is it?"

Lindsay bristled. It seemed he was determined to

think of her as a spoiled jet-setter. "I told you I was prepared to help," she replied coolly, to which Philip laughed out loud.

"Oh, you are, are you? Well, we'll see."

Back at the winery, Philip ushered Lindsay into a huge room filled with barrels, some very large, others small, reaching almost to the ceiling.

"This is where we age the vintage," Philip explained. "Our regular reds go directly from the large redwood tanks to bottle. Over there, those smaller, sixty-gallon French oak barrels hold our special wines, the varietals. I don't know how much you know about—"

"Inia told me about your plans," Lindsay put in quickly.

Philip shook his head. "Not much goes on around here that Inia doesn't know about." He pointed to the smaller casks. "The varietals are stored in these barrels because they mature faster when they have more surface to act against. We age them here for about two to two and a half years before they're bottled. Then they continue to age in the bottle for as long as twenty more years if desired. After this year's harvest we'll open the first bottles to sample. Then we'll know if we've succeeded or not."

"Inia said that if they fail you might have to sell Kia Ora."

His jaw tightened. "If they fail we'll have no choice. I've had to borrow heavily over the past ten years to finance the project."

Lindsay spoke carefully, for she knew by now how much Kia Ora meant to Philip, *and*, she realized ruefully, how much it was coming to mean to her. Still, it was best to face the matter realistically and at least examine all the options. It would be a tragedy to see a hundred years of tradition end in bankruptcy.

"If what Inia tells me is true, perhaps it would be best to sell now," she told him gently. "At least then you'd have the cash to start again."

Philip flushed slightly beneath his deep tan.

"And *you'd* have the cash to run back to your swinging Hollywood friends," he spat at her bitterly. "Let's see, your share from the sale of Kia Ora would keep you quite nicely for several years at least, even in the style you and Alex were accustomed to." His look was scathing. "And you wouldn't even have to dirty your dainty little hands."

"Why, you impossible—egotistical—" But Lindsay saw she was talking to the air. Philip had already turned his back and was walking in long, impatient strides toward the door.

"Come on," he said brusquely. "I'll show you the crushing room."

They moved in silence into a room that was almost as large as the aging room. A short, stocky man in his early forties with reddish gray hair and a stiff mustache was directing two men as they hosed out a large steel machine that Philip called a crusher-stemmer.

"This is Rudy Corrigan, my cellarmaster," Philip said curtly.

The Irishman's rough, red face broke into a wide grin. "So you're Alex's wife. The men were tellin' me a beautiful young lady had arrived last night. Now I see that they weren't exaggeratin' any. Well, what do you think of the place?"

Lindsay, still fuming from the exchange in the aging room, forced herself to return the cellarmaster's smile. "It's rather difficult to absorb it all in one morning," she answered stiffly, thinking that her words carried more truth than the little man would understand.

"Ah, but this is the best time of year to be learnin'.

We start the harvest soon and there'll be so much goin' on it'll make your head spin."

"I'm already a little dizzy, Rudy," Lindsay answered honestly. "I had no idea so much went into making wine."

"It's an art, no doubt about it," the gnomelike man replied with a grin. "But then for those of us who've been at it most of our lives, there's nothin' quite like it. Once winemakin's in your blood it's helpless you are to break away."

Lindsay wondered about the cellarmaster's words as she made her way back to the house, having excused herself from Philip's company as soon as they'd left Rudy. The joy she'd felt during the early part of the tour had turned to a slow-burning fury. How could Philip be so antagonistic toward her, and so presumptuous about her former life-style? He, who had driven some poor woman to take her life ten years ago. How dare he stand in judgment?

Lindsay thought of Philip and Alex and her husband's abrupt departure from Kia Ora. Despite a few superficial similarities the two cousins were virtually opposite in every way. Whereas Philip loved the vineyard, Alex had hated it so much that in four years of married life together he never once mentioned its existence. Alex's irresponsibility and wanderlust must have caused his father and Philip no end of grief. Still, Philip's obvious animosity seemed to go beyond this. It was almost a personal vendetta, directed first at Alex, and now, through no fault of her own, toward her. Once again Lindsay wondered what could have happened between the two cousins all those years ago.

Even before she reached the kitchen she could hear their voices, Inia's deep and irritated, the man's softer, almost timid. Occasionally, Kiri's higher voice would come between the two, protesting in a disagreeable whine. As Lindsay came within sight of the kitchen, she saw a dark, sturdy young man in work clothes talking to the two women in the doorway. The man looked up self-consciously as Lindsay came closer and, with a quick word to Inia, started to leave.

"No, Michael, stay for a moment," the housekeeper told him. "I want you to meet Alex's wife, Lindsay Macek. Miss Lindsay, this is Michael Taira, a friend of Kiri's. Michael works here on the vineyard."

Michael smiled and hesitantly accepted the hand which Lindsay offered. She realized that this must be Kiri's young man, the one her mother was so anxious for her to marry. As she studied Michael's strong build and clear, honest brown eyes she felt the girl could do a good deal worse.

"I'm very pleased to meet you, Michael," she told him sincerely. "Kiri has told me some nice things about you."

Michael shuffled in embarrassment, but Lindsay could see that he was pleased. And there was no doubting the pleasure on Inia's broad face. Only Kiri looked unhappy, and she rudely excused herself from the room.

"I'm glad you're back from the winery," Inia told Lindsay, ignoring her daughter's abrupt departure. "I've packed a picnic lunch for you and Stephie. She's out of school early today and I thought the two of you might like to go to the beach. Michael can drive you over in the truck."

Lindsay hardly knew what to say. While her plans for the afternoon were not definite, she had hoped for a chance to prove her worth around the vineyard.

Then, for the first time, she noticed Stephanie

sitting quietly at the kitchen table, her solemn eyes wide as she listened to the adults. Why, she really wants to go, Lindsay realized suddenly. She must be terribly lonely at Kia Ora with no friends her own age. And with everyone at the vineyard so busy at this time of year her outings must be limited. If Lindsay refused to go she might be losing a valuable opportunity to make friends with the child. And for some reason she wanted very much to gain Stephanie's confidence.

"What a wonderful idea, Inia," she said, winking at Stephanie. "I love the ocean. And I've heard that New Zealand has some of the most beautiful beaches in the world." She looked at the little girl expectantly. "Would you really show them to me, Stephanie?"

The child darted a fearful look at Inia, then bashfully nodded her head.

Inia's low voice boomed through the kitchen. "Good," she said, pleased. "Now hurry up and change. Michael has too much to do around here to stay at the beach with you, but I promise to send him back before tea." She held up a large wicker basket. "Everything you need is in here. Now scoot, both of you."

The drive to the coast was beautiful. They passed through the town of Henderson, then continued on around an inner bay that lay between two peninsulas on the upper Waitemata Harbour. Auckland, rising between the Pacific Ocean and the Tasman Sea, spread out in gently rolling hills and valleys.

"The city was built on many extinct volcanoes," Michael explained as they passed through the toll gates on the northern side of the Harbour Bridge. "It is New Zealand's largest city and contains nearly a quarter of the country's population. The beaches are usually crowded at this time of year, but I know a little cove not too far from Mairangi Bay where you won't have to jostle with tourists.''

Michael turned off the road and soon pulled the truck over to a grass-fringed area near the sand.

"I'll be back to pick you up before tea," he told them, and after settling them on the beach, he drove off in the truck.

Lindsay laid out the generous contents of the wicker basket on the wide blanket Inia had remembered to include. Delicious, thick beef sandwiches, hard-cooked eggs, *tamarillo*, a local tree tomato, and excellent slices of blue vein cheese made Lindsay realize how hungry she was despite the enormous breakfast she'd consumed. At the bottom of the basket she found an assortment of fresh fruit and the inevitable bottle of wine, this time a fine Beaujolais. For Stephanie, Inia had packed lemonade, icy cold and tart.

As they enjoyed their feast, Lindsay noticed that the child had brought along a colorful beach ball in a canvas tote bag.

"Do you like to play ball?" she asked, hoping to bridge the awkward silence which had engulfed them since Michael's departure.

Stephanie shook her head slightly, her dark blue eyes lowered intently onto her food. "Inia packed it," she said softly.

"I see. But you don't care to play."

Again the slight nod of the dark head.

"What would you like to do then?"

The child answered without looking up. "I'm going to build a sand castle."

Stephanie's words held no invitation for Lindsay to join her, and they finished their lunch in silence. When they were through, Lindsay packed away the leftovers and watched the child position herself near the water. Although there were several children around, Stephanie carefully chose a location well away from the others. It's almost as if she *wants* to be alone, Lindsay thought, yet she knew this was highly unlikely. Almost all the children she had dealt with professionally had had a healthy desire for the company of others their own age. A more likely explanation was that Stephanie had simply been alone too long. Adult company for a nine-year-old was fine, but not as a steady diet.

After their picnic area was tidied, Lindsay slipped off the white terry-cloth robe she wore over her bikini and was suddenly aware of the suit's very brief cut. Although the style had been fashionable at Beverly Hills poolsides, it seemed conspicuous here, and, as Lindsay stretched out on the blanket, she decided one of her first purchases would have to be a suit with a more suitable cut. That is, if she stayed. Practically speaking it would be much better for everyone if she left now, before she fell further in love with Kia Ora. Philip bitterly resented her intrusion into his life and would undoubtedly be relieved when she left. Still, she felt a disturbing reluctance to go home, a home which seemed more remote to her by the hour. Now when she thought of home it was a vision of an old, stately manor which came into her mind—tall trees— endless vines stretching out for miles—rolling, gentle hills—

Lindsay awoke with a start. Looking at her watch, she realized she had been asleep for almost half an hour. With a sudden, frightening jolt, she remembered Stephanie. She should have watched her more closely. What if the child had gotten into difficulty so close to the water's edge? Then, with tremendous relief, she spotted the gleaming head of black hair bobbing up and down as the little girl dug quietly in the moist sand. As she watched the child play, Lindsay was struck by how much she looked like her father. Stephanie's eyes were the same remarkable shade of cobalt, and her long, silky hair shone with identical blue-black highlights. But there was no sign of her father's confidence, his brash assurance of himself. The child looked sadly pathetic playing off by herself. Getting up, Lindsay walked over to her.

Stephanie looked up as Lindsay approached but said nothing, concentrating instead on an elaborate, turreted castle which she was forming out of moist sand. Her long braids were worn up today, wound several times around her small head like a sort of crown. Lindsay thought the effect very becoming.

"You look like a princess," she told her. Indeed, with her large dark eyes and perpetually solemn look she was very much like Princess Dagmar, from the play *The Princess Who Couldn't Laugh.* With sudden inspiration, Lindsay told Stephanie how the princess's ministers promised her hand in marriage to anyone who could make her smile but instant banishment to those who failed.

"Every morning loyal subjects lined up before the royal balcony to try to make the princess laugh. But no matter what they did she would bow her head and cry even harder than before." She watched Stephanie closely. Despite the child's apparent absorption with her building, Lindsay could tell she was listening carefully to the tale. Encouraged, she went on, letting the story build dramatically.

"Then one day, Hans, a handsome young fisherman, came to the palace to try his luck. Everyone before him had failed, even the funniest jesters in the land, and when the people saw Hans they jeered at him for even trying. But Hans had a secret. In his arms he carried a goose, a magic goose, given to him by the princess' fairy godmother. When the cook tried to snatch the goose away from Hans she stuck fast to it, and when others tried to help her they became stuck, too. Soon, everyone was following Hans around the courtyard in a kind of funny parade, even the animals, and for the first time in over a year the beautiful Dagmar was laughing. Naturally, because of his success, she and Hans were married and went on to live happily ever after."

Lindsay saw the barest flicker of a smile cross the girl's face.

"Have you ever seen a play, Stephanie?" she asked.

The little girl shook her head. "No, but Sara said I might go and see her sometime."

"Sara?"

"Sara is a friend of Papa's. She's an actress."

"And she's doing a play in the area?"

Stephanie nodded. "In Auckland. It's to open soon."

"Well, then, I'm sure your papa will take you to see it." She watched the child closely. "But how would you like to act in a play yourself? I mean actually play out a real part?"

Stephanie looked frightened and Lindsay went on in a hurry. "No, it's fun, really. I've acted in lots of plays and helped all sorts of children do it, too." She stood up. "Here, I tell you what. Why don't we pretend that you're the sad Princess Dagmar and I'll be the men who try to make her laugh."

The little girl looked doubtful.

"Come on," Lindsay coaxed, "You'll like it." She stood up and began an elaborate pantomime. Very soon, Stephanie was smiling, then laughing as Lindsay pranced about mimicking the antics of the characters in the story.

"No, no," Lindsay said, trying to look severe, "you're not suppose to laugh. The princess must cry until Hans comes in with the magic goose."

"I can't help it," the little girl said, near tears. "You're so funny."

"Well, remember, the princess in the play didn't think so," she admonished playfully.

For a long time the two acted out the drama, Lindsay doing her best to look ridiculous, Stephanie trying valiantly, but not too successfully, to be serious. Finally, after a crazy parade about the sand with Stephanie firmly attached to Lindsay's middle, the two collapsed into a heap, laughing hysterically.

"Oh, that *was* fun," Stephanie pronounced. "Let's do it again."

Lindsay sat up in the sand and shook her head. "No way, my dear *unsolemn* princess. That's enough playacting for one afternoon. Come on," she said, jumping to her feet. "I'll race you to the beach ball. Last one there gets a dunking!"

For nearly an hour the two romped in the sand, happily tossing the large plastic ball. Lindsay felt warmed by the sun and the exertion, but nothing warmed her heart like the sight of Stephanie's happy face. Now she's behaving like a real nine-year-old, Lindsay thought, delighted with her success. I must find some more plays for us to act out. It's wonderful therapy.

Then it happened. One minute she was reaching out to catch one of Stephanie's wilder throws, and the next she saw the sand castle just beneath her feet. In an effort to avoid smashing Stephanie's masterpiece, she swerved, twisting her right ankle painfully in the process. With a little cry, she fell to the sand.

"You'll never make the All Blacks," came a low voice from behind her.

Lindsay turned around, holding onto her throbbing ankle.

"What?" she said, talking through clenched teeth. Standing very tall behind her, tan against the white sand, was Philip Macek.

"I said you'll never make the All Blacks. They're our champion rugby team, so called because of the color of their uniforms. Every New Zealand boy dreams of making the team someday. You're obviously not in the competition." Philip's eyes traveled over her skimpily clad body. "Although, with that swimsuit, who knows? Is that the latest Hollywood fashion?" he asked dryly. "If it is, I must say that's one custom I approve."

Before Lindsay could answer, he stooped down and picked up her foot. "Let's see that ankle."

Lindsay felt a tingling warmth as his strong, rough hands made contact with her smooth skin. It was almost like an electric shock. She looked up quickly but read nothing in his face but polite concern.

"It doesn't look too serious," he said. "Still, it's a good thing I came by to get you instead of Michael." He rubbed her lower leg gently between his hands, causing Lindsay to hold her breath.

"I'm fine, really," she said, trying unsuccessfully to pull her foot away as his hands explored further up her leg.

"It's always best to be safe," he said, ignoring her efforts to break away. He turned to his daughter. "Run to the car and get the first-aid kit, will you, Peanut? We'll just bind this ankle to keep it steady."

"No, Stephanie," Lindsay cried out, "there's no need for that. I'll be fine in a minute."

The child hesitated, looking from her father to Lindsay, then ran off toward the road.

"I told you I'm fine," Lindsay said angrily. She couldn't be sure if her annoyance was caused by his authoritarian handling of the situation or the continued presence of his hands on her leg. "You're making too much of this." She tried wriggling her toes and stifled an involuntary wince. "See, there's hardly any pain now. I'll just try putting a little weight on it and I'm sure—"

As Lindsay started to get up, Philip leaned over, blocking her body with his own. His hands, finally off her leg, were now in a much more precarious position just beneath her breasts.

"Really, I'm fine," she said breathlessly. "I want to get up—I—"

"You talk too much," Philip said huskily, coming uncomfortably close. Her protests were cut off as his lips brushed hers, lightly, tentatively. Then, with a sharp intake of breath, he claimed her mouth with a hungry insistence. She felt his hard, lean body as he pulled her up against his chest. His eager tongue parted her lips, probing her mouth, exploring every corner with unexpected urgency and causing erratic flames of desire to course through her body under his touch. One of his hands brushed aside the flimsy material of her suit to cup a breast, massaging it gently, persistently. Horrified at her own response, she fought to pull away, to be free of his crushing lips, his invading hands, but she was powerless to move.

Then, suddenly, with one fluid motion, Philip was off her, sitting as he had been before with her injured foot in his hands. Looking up, Lindsay saw Stephanie running toward them carrying a small metal box. She quickly rearranged her suit, then tried, less successfully, to calm her racing pulse. Surely the child would see that something had happened, that things were not as they had been. But Stephanie appeared only concerned with Lindsay's foot and watched solicitously as her father carefully bound the injured ankle with a stretch bandage. Catching his eye during the ministrations, Lindsay caught him looking at her, too, his expression puzzled. Then, as they made eye contact, his face changed and was suddenly controlled again, smoothly indifferent. Angrily, Lindsay wished she could turn off her own emotions as quickly, especially when they were so unwelcome.

The ride home in the Land Rover was strained. Only Stephanie appeared unaware of the tension riding with them, and after babbling on most uncharacteristically about their afternoon, she fell sound asleep on the back seat. For the remainder of the ride Philip was silent while Lindsay grappled with her own turbulent emotions. Now that it was over she was angry, furious that he could have been so brazen, and, she admitted uncomfortably, so downright confusing. This morning he had berated her for her frivolous life-style; then, only a few hours later, he was taking unbelievable liberties. But if she was upset with Philip Macek, she was appalled by her own treasonous response to his touch, horrified at the unbidden longing, so long dormant, which had risen up to assail her senses. She should have done something, anything, to stop him.

It was only when they were pulling up to the house that she realized she could hardly have screamed out with Stephanie so close by. Still, if it ever happened again— But that was impossible, Lindsay told herself sharply. The episode had meant nothing to Philip. She'd been an interesting diversion, nothing else. It would not be repeated. But what if it were—?

For the first time since she'd left Alex almost two years ago, Lindsay was not sure she could truthfully answer that question.

3

The next few days passed slowly. At Inia's insistence, although not without protest, Lindsay was settled in the sitting room and told firmly to stay off her feet. Despite her immobility, however, she was determined not to lose any ground where Stephanie was concerned. Every afternoon after school the little girl trotted into the sitting room to report on the day's happenings. Then they would go through the fine old books Lindsay had ferreted out of the basement and lose themselves in the wonderful world of make-believe, happily taking turns with all the parts and enjoying themselves immensely.

The best thing to come out of their afternoons together was the remarkable change in Stephanie's behavior at school. The names of new friends popped frequently into their conversations and Stephanie confided that one of them, Jenny, would soon be invited over to spend the night—a belated first, Lindsay surmised. The biggest surprise of all was Stephanie's plan to try out for a part in the school play next week, an event she had previously referred to with horrified awe. She and Lindsay went over the part until the child knew the lines from memory and could give a very passable interpretation to the role.

The playacting was fun, but, more important, it took Lindsay's mind off Philip, if only for a little while. Since the incident at the beach she'd been able to think of little else. Again and again she felt the pressure of his lips on hers, his rough, probing hands exploring, teasing. Then, to her horror, her body would respond, unbidden, to the memory. Long forgotten desires were all too vividly remembered now, even more insistent than they had been with Alex. It was only when she reminded herself of Philip's motives, of his unbelievable audacity, that they were stilled, and then never for long. For days Lindsay felt as if she was on an emotional teeter-totter, with her common sense waging a losing battle with her physical longings.

And, of course, the forced confinement was not helping. Lindsay, active by nature, listened in mounting frustration to the busy sounds coming from the winery. More than anything, she longed to pitch in and help, to show Philip that she wasn't just a spoiled little rich girl. But getting past Inia was a Herculean task, and one she knew she was not up to yet.

Lindsay saw very little of Philip during those days. It was almost as if he were trying to erase his indiscretion on the beach by avoiding her completely. He always seemed to be gone before she came down in the morning, and was present only once for dinner. Even then he seemed distracted and the table conversation lagged painfully. For a while Lindsay attributed this preoccupation to the upcoming harvest, until a chance comment by Kiri one afternoon set her reeling.

"Sara Warner's the most glamorous woman I've ever seen," Kiri said dreamily as she moved a duster perfunctorily over the sitting room furniture. "If I looked as good as she does, my modeling career would be set."

"Stephanie tells me she's opening in a play soon."

Kiri ceased all pretense of working and sat down on the couch next to Lindsay. "She is. This Friday night. She's playing the lead in *Hedda Gabler* at the Meade Theatre in Auckland. Miss Warner's been terribly busy getting ready for opening night, which is why Mr. Philip has been out so late these past few nights."

Ridiculously, Lindsay's heart sank at the news. How naive she'd been to think that Philip's only interest was his vineyard. He was a healthy, robust male, and, God knows, not lacking in appeal. Of course he would be surrounded by interested women. Hadn't Kiri implied as much on that first day when she'd shown her to her room? But why in the world should it bother her? What concern was it of hers if he had an entire harem at his feet?

Still, when she spoke, she knew her voice was strained. "They sound like very good friends."

"Oh, they're practically engaged," the girl confided. "Miss Sara's the daughter of Matthew Warner, who runs the big cattle spread just west of Kia Ora. It's one of the largest and most prosperous ranches on North Island. He and Mr. Philip's father were old friends, so I guess it's only natural that their children should get together. Everyone expects Miss Sara and Mr. Philip to make the big announcement at this year's harvest celebration."

"Harvest celebration?"

"After the last grapes have been picked, Mr. Philip gives a big party for all the workers and their families. It's been a tradition ever since Mr. Philip's great-grandfather started Kia Ora almost a hundred years ago." The girl's eyes gleamed. "You'll love it, Miss Lindsay. There's music and dancing, and they always open some of the best wine to sample."

"Which this year will be the varietals."

"The new wines, yes. I don't know why everyone's so worried about them. Kia Ora wines are always good."

"I think Mr. Philip is hoping they'll be a little better than just 'good,' Kiri. He's counting on them being superior."

But Kiri was hardly listening. Her primary interest was obviously the celebration. "Kia Ora's parties are known all over the Henderson Valley," she went on. "A lot of people will come; other vintners and their workers, perhaps even Mr. Philip's friends from Auckland. Of course, Miss Sara will be there, and maybe some of the cast of the play. Mama's making me a new dress." She stood up and danced around the room, and Lindsay was struck by the grace and beauty of the girl's movements. "It will be cut straight to here, and the sleeves will drape over the shoulders like this," she said, moving her hands to illustrate the words. "And then the skirt will flare out in yards and yards of material. Mama refuses to cut the top properly," she pouted. "She says the pattern's too low for a girl my age." Kiri made a face. "As if I'm still a child. Well, I'll soon show her, when I leave this dreary place and start modeling."

"Won't you miss Michael when you leave?" Lindsay asked.

Kiri shrugged. "A little, maybe. But I'm sure I'll soon be too busy to worry about things like that. In fact, as soon as I get a chance I'm going to ask Miss Sara if she can help me get a job in the city."

On Thursday, Lindsay finally quit the sitting room couch. Not even the stubborn Inia could dispute that the ankle had completely healed and that further immobility was unnecessary. Then, that afternoon, Stephanie came bounding home to announce that they had been invited to the opening of Sara's play on Friday night. The little girl was very excited. Her anticipation seemed all the more heightened because of her recent exposure to the world of the theater.

"It will be a *real* play, Lindsay," she said, "not just one of the pretend ones we do. They'll even wear costumes, won't they?"

"Absolutely," Lindsay laughed. She paused and rummaged through one of her suitcases. "As a matter of fact, we put on *Hedda Gabler* at our school last year. Here," she said, pulling out a paperback volume, "I believe it's included in this anthology." She thumbed through the pages. "Yes, here it is. Do you know anything about the play?"

The little girl shook her head.

"Well, you'll enjoy the performance a lot more if you know what it's about. Why don't we read through it today? You can be Hedda and I'll take the other roles."

By Friday afternoon, Stephanie knew every nuance of the play and was almost beside herself with anticipation. She danced happily through Lindsay's bedroom, modeling dress after dress in an effort to choose just the right one for her first visit to the theater. Finally, they decided on a powder blue dress, which Stephanie decided had the most "grown-up" cut and Lindsay thought looked best with the child's dark blue eyes.

"Now, what are *you* going to wear?" the little girl asked.

Lindsay hesitated. She knew Stephanie assumed she would be going with them to the play, and she wasn't quite sure how to explain that she had no intention of socializing with Philip Macek. Lindsay intended to make sure that her only contacts with the vintner from now on were strictly business.

"I'm sorry, honey," she told Stephanie. "I don't think I'll be able to go. But you'll have a wonderful time. You can come home and tell me all about the play."

The child's eyes grew large. "But you have to go," she cried. "It wouldn't be any fun without you."

"Don't be silly, Stephie," Lindsay said. "Of course you'll have fun. Besides, this is a good chance for you and your dad to do something special, just the two of you."

"But we'd much rather have you with us," came the familiar voice from the doorway.

Stephanie went running to her father. "Oh, yes, Papa, please tell Lindsay she has to go with us. She knows everything about plays. It wouldn't be the same without her."

"I was trying to explain to Stephie that I can't possibly—"

Philip turned those remarkable eyes on Lindsay. "Of course you'll come," he interrupted. "An opening night in Auckland may not be as glamorous as a Hollywood premiere, but I think I can promise you an interesting evening. Besides, Stephanie is counting on it."

While, of course, my coming means nothing to you, Lindsay thought angrily, resenting his continual references to her former life. Then, at the sight of Stephanie's earnest face, she weakened. After all, did it matter what Philip Macek thought? This was Stephanie's big night and she really did want to share it with her. "All right," she said, confining her smile to the little girl, "I'll be happy to go."

"Hurray!" Stephanie cried. "Now we have to pick out your dress." She went to the closet and after a moment pulled out a bright red dress in the softest of fabrics. "I think she should wear this one, don't you, Papa?"

"I don't think so," Lindsay said quickly. "Perhaps something else." The red Qiana had been one of Alex's favorites, low cut and very soft and clinging. It had never failed to cause a sensation the few times she had worn it. She hardly knew now why she had brought it along on the trip. But certainly it was not what she had in mind for tonight.

Philip took the dress from his daughter and held it up in front of Lindsay. "I think you're right, Peanut," he said. "This dress should do nicely." His eyes raked thoroughly over Lindsay's trim figure, then rested on her small, oval face and large brown eyes. She knew the deep ruby color of the dress provided the perfect accent for her smooth, honey-toned complexion and fair hair, yet she was reluctant to concede to his demands.

Philip tossed the dress onto the bed, and she realized that as far as he was concerned the subject was closed. "Now that that's settled," he went on presumptuously, "I want the two of you ready early. I thought we'd dine out tonight before the theater." He winked at his daughter. "What do you say to that, Peanut?"

The little girl clapped her hands in glee. "Can we really, Papa? Oh, this is going to be the most exciting night of my whole life."

* * *

The Meade Theater was small but surprisingly well appointed. Lindsay was pleased to see that they had been given excellent seats with a splendid view of the stage. Stephanie, animated all evening, was now looking around with ill-concealed impatience. To her chagrin, there were still several minutes to wait until curtain time.

Lindsay wished she could be as enthusiastic. Their dinner, although excellent, had nonetheless been laden with an undercurrent of tension, relieved only by Stephanie's constant stream of chatter. The restaurant Philip had chosen, tucked into a little corner of the Auckland waterfront, was done in authentic Empire-period decor. Under any other circumstances, Lindsay would have relished the exquisitely prepared dishes and the really spectacular view of the harbor. But Philip's cool presence created an oppressive pall, and Lindsay nibbled only perfunctorily at the rich *toheroa* soup and tasty Bluff oysters scooped from the chilly waters of Foveaux Strait, fighting to remain civil for Stephie's sake.

Not that Philip hadn't been the perfect host. He had pointed out places of interest on the way to Auckland, advised them about the meal and seated them solicitously in the theater. Only a certain remoteness where she was concerned kept intruding on the evening, making it impossible for Lindsay to truly relax. Several times she wished she hadn't come along, for it was obvious that he had only asked her for his daughter's sake and was uncomfortable in her presence. Then, seeing Stephanie's beaming face, she realized she had done the right thing. It was worth anything to see the child blossom into such a beautiful flower.

At last the curtain rose, and Lindsay heard Stephanie's satisfied gasp as the interior of the Tesman home was revealed. How much more the set means to the child, Lindsay thought, now that she knows what drama will enact itself there. Sneaking a look at her, she saw Stephanie examining the dark porcelain stove where later Hedda would cruelly burn Lovborg's manuscript, and the small room in the back where the play would climax with Hedda's suicide.

Lindsay watched eagerly for Sara Warner to make her entrance, for she knew that only the most sensitive actress could successfully portray the bewilderingly complex Hedda Gabler. And she was not disappointed. With a flurry of skirts, Hedda burst upon the stage, immediately taking possession of it, dominating the play and the other characters so skillfully that they really came to life only in their relationship to her.

In the next seat, Lindsay could see that Stephanie was captivated by the play, and, looking beyond the child, she saw that Philip was keenly intent on the drama as well. His dark eyes followed the graceful Hedda about the stage, almost oblivious of the other actors. Quite irrationally, Lindsay's heart sank at his preoccupation with Sara Warner. Well, why shouldn't he be engrossed, she told herself sternly, remembering her talk with Kiri. It must be very satisfying to watch someone you love give such a beautiful performance.

Then, as the play progressed, Lindsay gradually forgot everything else as the drama weaved its spell on the audience. She sympathized with George Tesman, worried for Lovborg and felt pity for poor Mrs. Elvsted, superbly played by a young, blond actress of startling intensity. The climactic scene, dramatic and extremely well played, caused shock, then momentary silence before the theater erupted in wild applause. As the last of the ovation subsided, Lindsay felt Philip's hand on her arm.

"Stephanie tells me you're an expert," he said, leading her out of the aisle. "What's the verdict?"

Lindsay searched for the right words. While Sara Warner's portrayal of Hedda was not quite in a league with Duse, Campbell or Nazimova, it was, nonetheless, a notable performance. "It was excellent," she pronounced. "A really top-notch production. But I'm hardly an expert."

Philip looked down at her derisively. "Oh, but I think you are." His hand brushed along her back as he guided her through the crowded foyer toward the back of the theater.

"We've been invited to the opening night cast party," Philip explained, reading Lindsay's inquiring look. "Stephanie can stay long enough to meet the actors, and then I've asked Michael Taira to come take her home."

A large room behind the stage had been set up with bright crepe streamers and other colorful decorations. Already, hordes of first-nighters were clustered around the members of the cast with noisy congratulations and free-flowing champagne. Stephanie was subdued for the first time that evening as she looked from one actor to the other in the crowded room.

The first person they met was the director, John Maclennan, a heavy man of medium height with a florid, mottled complexion. As he rushed over to greet them it was obvious he was still riding the crest of the tumultuous ovation which had met his production.

"Well, well, Macek," he said loudly, clapping Philip heartily on the back, "what did you think of our little show? Rather a smashing performance by Sara, wasn't it?"

"It should be for the amount of time you rehearsed her," Philip answered dryly.

"Oh, come on now, old fellow," Maclennan said,

undaunted. "That's necessary and you know it. Now, tell me what you really thought of it."

"It was very good," Philip said. Then he nodded to Lindsay. "But this is our resident expert—Lindsay Macek, John Maclennan. She knows a lot more about it than I do, and she has already pronounced Hedda an unqualified success."

"Splendid!" the director shouted. "You've got good taste, young lady. Of course, the end of the second act dragged a bit. That's always a tricky scene to pull off. But, all in all, I'd say you're right. It was an unqualified success!" He took Lindsay by the arm. "Now, come over here, both of you, oh, and you, too, Stephanie. I want you to meet some of the cast."

The next several minutes were spent in a whirlwind of introductions, until, finally, John Maclennan left them to their own devices. "Now you mingle while I see what's holding up the next wave of champagne," he told them. "It wouldn't do for the party to dry up this early. You know everyone, Philip. Move around and give people a chance to meet this charming young lady."

Uncomfortable without John Maclennan's congenial presence, Lindsay was about to suggest that she accompany Stephanie home early when they were accosted by the actor who had played George Tesman.

"So this is the budding actress," he said to Stephanie. Roger Nicolson, appearing taller and several years younger than he had onstage, took the little girl's hand and raised it gallantly to his lips, "Your father has told us all about you. Perhaps someday I will have the honor of playing opposite you, my dear Miss Macek."

Lindsay had to smile as the little girl blushed deeply, but it was obvious she was very pleased with the attention.

"Oh, I'd love that, Mr. Nicolson," she said, wide-eyed. "But I haven't even been in my first play yet. Lindsay is still teaching me."

The actor's eyes traveled beyond Stephanie's head and rested appreciatively on Lindsay, seeming not to miss a single curve under the frothy red dress.

"Ah, so you're the visitor to our fair island." He looked reproachfully at Philip. "You neglected to tell me that your cousin was so beautiful. No wonder you've been hiding her away on that vineyard of yours."

Philip smiled, but Lindsay suspected he was not pleased.

"I'm hardly hiding her away, Roger. Unfortunately, Lindsay suffered a slight accident on the beach earlier in the week and was off her feet for a few days."

"Ah, but I can see that she is most delightfully back on them now," the actor said, frankly taking in Lindsay's slim ankles. "Please allow me to get you some champagne, my dear. You have to help us celebrate our humble opening."

"It was hardly humble," Lindsay laughed. "You know as well as I do that it was a brilliant success."

"So it was," agreed the actor, immodestly. "But I'd much rather hear someone else say it, especially a lovely young woman. An actor's ego is boundless, my dear. We are in constant need of adoration and appreciation."

As Roger moved off toward the bar, a stunning woman with rich auburn hair and clear, emerald-green eyes grasped Philip by the arm. "There you are, darling," she said, turning an exquisitely sculptured face for him to kiss. Lindsay thought that Kiri had been right: Sara Warner was the most glamorous woman she had ever seen. Her dark red hair was a mass of carefully arranged curls, which provided an elegant frame for her perfect features. The green, thickly fringed eyes flashed eagerly as she looked up into Philip's face. She was not only beautiful but also carried herself with an air of complete self-possession. She was commanding and at the same time infinitely graceful. No wonder she has such presence as Hedda Gabler, Lindsay thought. The woman is a born actress. And no wonder Philip had eyes for no one else on the stage. With Sara around, everyone else pales by comparison.

"I've been looking all over for you," Sara smiled. "And you did bring Stephanie after all."

"Only for a little while, Sara," Philip said, resting his hand lightly on Stephanie's shoulder. "One of my men will be picking her up as soon as she's met everyone."

Stephanie was looking up at the actress with obvious adoration. "You were wonderful," she told her softly. "And so was the play."

Sara laughed, a full, earthy laugh that caught the attention of several groups. "Darling, how sweet. If only the critics are as kind. But you couldn't have understood very much of it, I'm afraid."

"Oh, but Stephanie has read the play through several times," Lindsay said. "I think she has a very good grasp of what Ibsen was trying to say."

For the first time Sara Warner really looked at Lindsay, and although her smile remained just as open, Lindsay thought she detected a measure of wariness cross her lovely face. But her voice, when she spoke, was gracious.

"You must be Philip's cousin. Philip, she's charming. You really should have brought her around before this."

"I'm sure you'll be seeing more of her now that she knows her way into town," Philip said offhandedly. "Lindsay is used to far more exciting fare than we can offer her at Kia Ora."

For Stephanie's sake, Lindsay bit back a retort, but she was stung by Philip's remark.

"Then we'll look forward to your visits." Sara wound graceful hands through Philip's arm. "I'm sorry," she said, flashing a devastating smile at Lindsay and the child, "but I really must steal Philip away from you for a few minutes. I've promised no end of people I'd introduce them to New Zealand's most famous vintner." She squeezed his arm affectionately. "You'll forgive me for snatching him away, won't you? I promise to return him intact before you know it."

"I see you've met Sara," a voice said at her elbow. Roger Nicolson handed Lindsay a bubbling glass of wine and Stephanie a larger one of punch. He watched the actress and Philip as they moved to a group of people by the bar. "They make a rather striking couple, don't they? They've become quite an item."

Lindsay found her throat suddenly dry. "Yes, they do," she agreed tightly, annoyed by her totally unwelcome reaction to his words. She took a quick sip of champagne. "Miss Warner really does make a wonderful Hedda," she went on, anxious to change the subject.

"She does indeed," agreed the actor. "Very talented is our Sara." Roger drew his hands through Lindsay's and Stephanie's arms. "Come on now, ladies. Allow me to show you off. It's not every day I have the privilege of escorting two such beautiful women."

Within the half hour Michael Taira came for Stephanie, and very reluctantly the child allowed herself to be packed off for home.

"We'll talk about it tomorrow," Lindsay promised her, kissing her lightly on the cheek. "Maybe we can even act it out again. This time we'll know how the real actors did it."

The cast party continued for several more hours until at last someone suggested they wait out the reviews over breakfast. Lindsay had spent most of the time with Roger Nicolson, whom she found to be surprisingly good company. For all his affectations, Roger was nonetheless a witty, considerate companion, and since Philip had done little more than cast an occasional glance in her direction all evening, Lindsay was grateful for this attention.

They had breakfast at a little restaurant, well known to everyone but Lindsay, just around the corner from the theater. At four o'clock John Maclennan rushed in with the early edition of the morning paper.

"It's a hit," he cried, slapping down papers on every table he passed. "Even that old cynic Woodbridge gave us a good review."

Maclennan paused dramatically. "Boys and girls—we're in!"

Lindsay was surprised to see that they would not be going back to Kia Ora in the Land Rover.

"I had Taira drive over in the Aston Martin," Philip explained, starting the engine of the sleek black sports car. "I want to show you something on the way home."

As they drove, Lindsay leaned her head back against the snow-white upholstery, surprisingly relaxed. The evening, despite Philip's evasions, had been fun, mostly because of Roger Nicolson. He had been charming and entertaining, and Lindsay knew she would seriously consider his invitation to come to dinner some time next week.

As she gazed up at the stars fading rapidly in the lightening sky, she wondered again about Philip's relationship with Sara Warner. If, as Kiri said, they were practically engaged, the actress must surely resent Philip's polite, albeit desultory, attention to his cousin's widow. What did she think of Alex's wife appearing after all these years? Then, as Philip maneuvered the car up a spiral road leading to the top of Mount Eden, she quickly stopped thinking about the actress and gave all her attention to the hundreds of lights flickering below.

"You're sitting on the top of a volcano," Philip told her casually, then laughed at her startled expression. "Don't worry, it's extinct. But it is the highest point in Auckland. And in a few minutes you're going to see something unforgettable."

Only moments later the sky brightened as the sun peered over the horizon. All around them a panoramic view was illuminated in the cool, shimmering light of daybreak. With just a turn of her head Lindsay could see the two oceans bordering North Island, the Tasman Sea and the Pacific Ocean. Below them buildings and parks seemed to wait expectantly for the new day and in the distance she could see the Waitakere Ranges magically appear like fresh images on a developing photo.

"It's beautiful," she said softly.

When Philip remained silent, she turned to catch him staring at her intently, a puzzled expression on his tan face. Then, without a word, he leaned over and took her chin in one hand while the other circled her slim waist.

"So are you," he said, his mouth so close that their breath intermixed.

Gently he touched her lips, just a sweeping brush that left her breathless.

"No, don't," she gasped, fighting the tide of emotion that threatened to drown her control.

Heedlessly, he drew her to him, and his insistent lips parted hers, his tongue once again probing against their moist softness. Lindsay knew she should break away, put an end to this madness now, before she succumbed any further. But already an intoxicating excitement coursed through her as she felt her body coming vibrantly to life under his touch. Rebelliously, her arms refused to resist what her shameless senses most desired. With an abandonment that she decried even as she surrendered, she pressed her body tighter against his muscular chest and let her hands pull his head closer, his mouth harder into hers. It had been so long—so long—and her appetite, now whetted, responded more fiercely than it ever had before. Never had she craved a man like this, longed for his touch, his love, his body.

Then as her lips moved against his with unrestrained need, Philip suddenly pulled away, leaving Lindsay dizzy and confused. His knuckles were almost white as he started the little car and Lindsay could sense the tension in his taut body as he whipped the car around and sent it spinning down the mountain. When they reached the base of Mount Eden, he glanced at her before they turned onto the main road.

"You really are full of surprises," he said, his voice thick and barely controlled. "I know what your little game is, but it isn't going to work. My uncle invested his life in that land, and my investment cannot be less. Your husband did his best to destroy the vineyard, and

I'm not going to let you do the same." With a shuddering grinding of gears, he sent the sports car leaping into motion.

"No matter how desirable you are, or how damn much I want you, no wife of Alex Macek is going to tempt me into selling Kia Ora."

4

Later, in her room, Lindsay found sleep impossible. After two hours of fitful tossing, she tried instead to wash away her restlessness with a cold shower. Then, realizing nothing could dispel her tumultuous emotions, Lindsay decided to carry out the plan which had been forming since shortly after her arrival at Kia Ora. Quickly, she dressed in her oldest clothes, waited until she was sure Philip had left the house and ran lightly down the stairs into the front hall. There she found Kiri absently pushing a mop over the polished hardwood floor. Lindsay could see the girl had been crying.

"Kiri, what's the matter?" she asked in concern.

The girl shook her head. Then, as Lindsay took her hand, she burst into a flood of tears.

"Mama and I had a terrible fight last night," she cried. "She's forbidden me to talk anymore about being a model. She took all my magazines and burned them."

"But why? I know she wasn't happy with your plans, but they didn't seem to upset her to that extent."

"Michael asked me to marry him," the girl blurted out.

"And you don't want to."

Kiri hesitated. "I like Michael all right, but I just don't feel ready to get married." Her fingers unconsciously twisted a small corner of the apron. "I have to get out of Henderson. I have to at least try to make it on my own before I settle down."

Lindsay nodded, sympathetic to the girl's pressing need. "Then you must explain your feelings to Michael," she told her gently. "You have to make him understand why you aren't ready yet for that kind of commitment."

Kiri's dark brown eyes were huge. "But I don't want to hurt him. It's not his fault Mama's being so stubborn. She says I should marry him—that if I don't I'll be making a terrible mistake."

"Who knows, Kiri?" Lindsay told her gently. "Perhaps you *will* be making a mistake. But we all have to take a chance some time or other. In the end you can only do what you feel is best."

The girl's tears ebbed and her face brightened. "That's right, isn't it?" she said eagerly. "I have to think for myself now. It wouldn't be fair to say yes to Michael just to please Mama, would it?"

Lindsay brushed several wisps of shiny black hair from the girl's damp forehead. "That would certainly be a very poor way to start your life together, Kiri. A successful marriage depends on a great deal of mutual love and trust."

Kiri squeezed Lindsay's hand. "Oh, thank you, Miss Lindsay. You've really helped. Now I think I know what I have to do." With a final smile, the girl danced gracefully down the hallway, flinging off her apron as she went.

Well, at least she had helped someone this morning, Lindsay thought ruefully. If only she could settle her own problems as easily.

Peeking cautiously into the kitchen, Lindsay was relieved to find it empty. She was just not in the mood for one of Inia's early morning feasts. Instead, she poured a cup of coffee from the stove and hastily gulped it down before slipping out the back door and over to the winery. All around were signs of preharvest bustle as grape gondolas, crushers, tanks and presses were repaired, scrubbed and, in some cases, painted before the influx of the new vintage. More than a little bewildered by the flurry of activity, she set off to find the cellermaster, Rudy Corrigan. This time she discovered the little Irishman supervising a group of men in the aging room.

"So, you're back on your feet," he greeted, a broad grin on his rough race. "We thought maybe one day of our company had scared you off."

Lindsay felt immediately cheered by the honest, rough-hewn face. "Not at all. In fact, I couldn't wait to get back. I'm ready to go to work."

The little man looked surprised. "So, it's work your lookin' for, Mrs. Macek. And does Mr. Philip know you're plannin' to wear those pretty little hands of yours to the nubbin'?"

Lindsay hesitated, not quite sure how to field the question. "We've discussed the partnership, of course," she answered carefully. "And I've told him that I have every intention of pulling my share of the load."

Rudy's grin broadened. "Good for you, lass." He turned to the other workers. "Did you hear that, boys? We've got another Macek on our hands. And by the looks of her she's got a healthy bit of spunk for all her good looks." The Irishman swept a calloused hand around the large room. "And where do you fancy startin', Mrs. Macek?"

"First of all, I'd like you to call me Lindsay," she said, relieved that Rudy approved of her plan. "And I'd like to start wherever I can be the most use."

"All right." He grinned. "Miss Lindsay it is." The little man considered for a moment before going on. "Well, now, let me see. We can always use an extra hand at cleaning out the tanks." He looked at her doubtfully. "But it's a wet job, lass. Are you sure you don't mind sloshin' about in a bit of water?"

"I'm here to work, Rudy," she assured him. "If I get wet that's part of the job. Now, what do I do?"

"First, you put these on," Rudy said. He handed her a pair of knee-high rubber boots that looked several sizes too large. After these were on, the little man reached for an oversized towel and tied it around her slender waist. "You might as well be dressed for the job," he explained with his usual grin. With a minimum of fuss, the cellarmaster went on to explain the scrubbing operation, then, with gratifying confidence in her ability, left her alone to get on with the job.

After he left, Lindsay looked over the long row of tanks that were now her responsibility. She was uncomfortably aware that every eye in the aging room was upon her, even though, superficially, at least, the men seemed engrossed in their own work. Well, Lindsay thought with a sigh, she had no one but herself to thank for getting her into this. There was no choice now but to show them she could do the job. Turning on the hose and taking a firm grip on the coarse scrub brush, she bent to her work.

Two hours and seven tanks later, Lindsay had a

more practical understanding of Rudy's warning. She was completely soaked, inside and out, having sloshed a good deal of water into the loose-fitting boots as well. And after climbing into the casks in order to reach every corner, she felt as if her back had been kicked by a mule. Ruefully, she realized that her idle years with Alex had taken their toll. Gone were the days when she could rise at dawn, milk the cows and put in two hours' work on her parents' farm before making the long trek to school. But despite her soaked condition and the dull aches assaulting every part of her body, Lindsay was surprised to find she felt wonderful. It was good to work with her hands again, to know she was contributing something, no matter how small, to the operation of the vineyard.

"We must be boring you more than I realized."

Lindsay whirled around to find Philip Macek watching her from the aging-room door.

"I told you I intended to help," Lindsay said, conscious that she must look a mess.

"I'm not sure how much help it will be if you drown." Philip moved to take the hose and brush from her hands. "You can stop the charade now. You've properly impressed, *and* distracted, my men long enough. We're much too busy at this time of year for your little games. They may be all right where you come from, but here we have serious work to accomplish."

Lindsay caught her breath. "Why, you— How dare you insinuate I have ulterior motives! I have a vested interest in Kia Ora."

"Yes, and we both know what it is, don't we?

Lindsay could barely contain her temper. "Why do you persist in supposing you can second-guess my thoughts?"

"For the simple reason that you read like a book,

my dear Lindsay. A far denser man than I could see through your little act. We both know you came to Kia Ora for only one reason." He swept out a tan, muscular arm. "Why don't you simply admit it and be done with all this nonsense?"

"Why you're—you're impossible!" Lindsay sputtered angrily. "You're the most exasperating man I've ever met. You wouldn't know the truth if it hit you over the head."

Then, as several heads turned in their direction, she lowered her voice, although not its intensity. "You probably won't believe this, Mr. Macek, but I have a strong respect for family tradition. I came to Kia Ora because half of it belonged to Alex."

Philip's expression was contemptuous. "Very touching," he said with deceptive mildness. "And, now that you've completed your pilgrimage to the Alex Macek shrine, your conscience, if you really have one, should be delightfully appeased. You can return to your friends, successful in your role as the dutiful little widow."

Lindsay flushed. "And what if I don't want to return?" Suddenly, the plan that had never been far from her thoughts since her arrival at the vineyard tumbled recklessly out as she squared up to Alex's hateful cousin. "As a matter of fact, I've decided to stay on in New Zealand. Under the terms of your uncle's will half of Kia Ora belongs to me now. And like it or not I intend to assume active control of my share of this vineyard!"

After Philip was gone, Lindsay sank onto an overturned barrel. All of a sudden she was very tired; the lost sleep the night before, his inexcusable behavior toward her today, had all contributed to a dull, pulsating throb in her temples. His look a moment ago, before he turned and stormed from the room, had been withering. Why hadn't he said something, anything, in answer to her tirade? At least then she would know where she stood.

Wearily, Lindsay wiped a wet clump of hair from her eyes. Now that it was over, she had to admit that the outburst had surprised even her. True, the thought of staying at Kia Ora had occurred to her more than once, and the idea of leaving was becoming increasingly distasteful. It was amazing how attached she had become to Inia, Kiri, Rudy and the others in such a short time. And then, of course, there was Stephanie. Lindsay's heart warmed at the thought of the little girl. Yes, she would very much hate to leave. With a sigh, Lindsay realized that in all probability Philip's infuriating words had only hastened her inevitable decision.

She looked around the aging room—at the workers, intent on their chores, and at the dozens of stacked casks, the large barrels holding this year's vintage and the smaller ones which held the uncertain key to Kia Ora's future. She now knew that more than anything she wanted to be part of this life, to experience again working with her hands, with the soil, seeing the results of her labor grow and be fruitful. Slowly, inexorably, Lindsay realized, the vineyard had worked its way into her bloodstream, too, and, like Rudy Corrigan, she seemed equally helpless to break away.

Dinner was a strained affair, with only Stephanie's lively chatter cutting through the almost palpable tension. Philip was formally polite but no more, and Lindsay noticed he ate sparingly of the delicious *paua*, or New Zealand abalone, that Inia had prepared. As for herself, she realized she was merely moving food from one part of her plate to the other, finally bringing on an exasperated outburst from the housekeeper.

"What are we going to do with this girl?" Inia complained loudly to Philip. "She works at the vineyard all day and then picks at her food like a bird. At this rate she's gonna waste away into nothin'."

Philip looked unimpressed. "I'm sure Mrs. Macek knows how to take care of herself," he replied coolly. "She seems to have quite a penchant for doing as she pleases."

Lindsay fumed, but for Stephie's sake said nothing until they finally left the table. Then she tried to excuse herself from the customary coffee and chocolate in the den by pleading a headache. There seemed little point in dragging out the laborious evening in Philip's company. But again, Lindsay was thwarted by the stalwart housekeeper.

"You'll do no such thing," Inia told her sharply. "I'm not surprised you don't feel well after the paltry amount of food you ate." She prodded Lindsay toward the den. "Now, you get in there and have some of the special dessert I made for tonight. No more arguments."

Reluctantly, Lindsay followed Philip and Stephanie into the cozy room and seated herself in an overstuffed chair, while her companions took seats opposite her on the couch. Although she made a show of examining a large, excellent oil painting of Kia Ora's founder, Ljuba Macek, which hung over the fireplace, Lindsay was uncomfortably aware of Philip's eyes on her. She was relieved when Kiri fluttered into the room a few minutes later carrying a tray. Lindsay noticed that the girl looked much happier than she had at their meeting that morning. In fact, there was an excited sparkle in her dark eyes.

"Mama says you're to have this," Kiri told her, placing a large wedge of homebaked fruit pie topped with rich cream in front of Lindsay. "And she wants you to eat every bit of it."

Stephanie giggled as she cut into her own pie. "I'm glad Inia worries about you, Lindsay," she said, ready to place a large spoon full of cream into her mouth, "'cause now we get these yummy desserts every night."

Lindsay smiled fondly at the child but found herself unable to do more than dawdle over the delicious dessert.

"Tomorrow Inia says she's going to make brandied cheesecake in honor of Miss Sara's visit," the little girl prattled on. "What time is she coming, Papa?"

Philip sipped at his coffee before answering, but even when he spoke his eyes continued to rest on Lindsay. "Sometime after lunch, Peanut," he said. "There's no performance tomorrow evening, so Sara will be able to spend the whole day."

The little girl clapped her hands. "Oh, Lindsay, won't that be fun? Maybe she'll even playact with us."

"That would be nice," Lindsay replied, but she could not share the child's enthusiasm about the impending visit. For all Sara's apparent warmth, Lindsay sensed the actress's wariness toward her, her perplexity in categorizing Lindsay's relationship with Philip. Well, Sara's confusion was certainly understandable, Lindsay thought wryly. Even *she* wasn't entirely certain of her feelings toward the exasperating vintner. Glancing covertly at Philip, Lindsay wondered how much her decision to remain at Kia Ora had been influenced by him, by his continual intrusion into her thoughts, her dreams. As much as she willed herself to forget, she remembered all too vividly the warmth of

69

those full, sensuous lips on hers, the touch of his rough hands caressing, exploring, sliding over her body—

Lindsay quickly diverted her eyes as Philip looked up from his coffee. My God, she thought, what had gotten into her? The man was obnoxious and unbelievably opinionated. Not only that, he was practically engaged, and here she was fantasizing about what it would be like to make love to him. Lindsay felt a sudden need for some fresh air and, excusing herself, she made her way out of the house and into the moonlit garden.

Once outside, she breathed deeply of the cool night air, letting its pungent sweetness revitalize her ebbing spirit. Under no circumstance could she weaken now by giving in to totally irrational emotions. Her position here at Kia Ora must remain totally businesslike. She and Philip shared a common interest in the vineyard, but beyond that their personal feelings could not be allowed to intrude.

Lindsay went to sit by a cluster of clematis, their fragrant blossoms a latticework of white lace shimmering in the moonlight. Leaning her head back against the bench, she let the tranquility of the lovely garden work its magic. Gradually her aching muscles relaxed and the dull throb in her temples began to recede. She would not let Philip's relationship with the beautiful Sara Warner interfere with her determination to make a success of Kia Ora. She must not even think about it. Luckily, tomorrow she would be too busy to worry about the actress. So pleased was Rudy Corrigan with her work on the barrels, he had asked her to spend the next day helping him sterilize the fermenting tanks with sulfur. Then the cellarmaster had promised to give her a lesson in the subtle art of wine tasting in Kia Ora's well-stocked cellars. Lindsay closed tired eyes and listened to the plaintive call of a far-off Kiwi bird.

Yes, she would stay busy. It would work out, she told herself drowsily. As long as she could keep her emotions on an even keel—

"Dreaming of home?"

The words, spoken almost in Lindsay's ear, startled her out of her musings, and she opened her eyes to find Philip sitting beside her on the bench.

"I must have dozed off," she said rather inanely.

"That was obvious. You looked so peaceful I thought you might be thinking of California."

"And that's all it takes to induce tranquility?" Lindsay turned to face Philip and once again marveled at the strong, clean line of his profile, so clearly defined now in the moonlight. As his mouth twisted in a smile, she wished she could read more of his expression.

"I just thought you might miss your friends," he said offhandedly, "or your parents. You never talk about home. I know nothing about your family."

"My father is dead," Lindsay told him quietly. "My mother is remarried and she and my stepfather live at our old family home in Iowa. It's the house where I was born."

Philip raised a dark brow. "I didn't think that was done anymore—having babies at home, I mean. At least not in the States."

Lindsay smiled. "Normally it isn't. But in a blizzard, under two feet of snow, there's not much choice."

"So you come from the Midwest," he said, and Lindsay thought she caught a note of surprise in his low voice. "And as soon as you could you moved to the big city."

"I was very young and I fell in love," Lindsay explained. "After we were married we made our home in California."

"The little Iowa girl and the big Hollywood producer," he said derisively. "Right out of the storybooks."

71

Lindsay turned her face to him, acutely aware even through her anger of his dangerous proximity, his scent musky and blatantly male. "It was no fairy tale, Philip," she replied shortly. "My life with Alex was very real."

She felt a strong arm encircle her shoulders while Philip's other hand tilted her face upward, toward his. "As real as this?" he asked softly.

As his lips found hers, it was as if she had received an electric shock, igniting a trail of fire that flashed through her body, threatening to engulf her within its flames. His eager tongue parted her resisting lips, then boldly took possession of her moist mouth, exploring it leisurely, titillatingly, until she was sure her senses would explode.

Furious at her own mutinous reactions, Lindsay tried to pull away, but his kiss only became more intense, his tongue more daring. His fingers glided lightly along her shoulder, then down her bare arm, coming to rest just below her breast.

"Can anything be as real as this?" he demanded, and Lindsay shivered as his hands moved to the neckline of her thin dress and slowly, meticulously, unfastened each button, one by one.

"Philip, no," she groaned, but his mouth cut off all protest.

"What are you afraid of?" he whispered, and his hands moved dangerously lower, etching circles of fire through the thin fabric of her dress. "Of this?" he breathed, as his fingers stroked to life the warm, forbidden regions of her body. "Or this?" Lindsay moaned in ecstatic torture as his hands continued their exploration, massaging, teasing, tormenting, until her entire being longed for release.

Then his dark head bent as his lips sought the

smooth, shadowed line of her throat, moving leisurely, agonizingly downward to brush aside the last remaining obstacles to his goal. With his teeth, he gently teased a sensitive nipple until it grew taut, revealing all too clearly her response to his touch.

"Philip, please—"

"Your words tell me no, but the rest of you is begging me to go on," he breathed, and an invading hand slid into the open front of her dress, warm and sensually abrasive against the cool softness of her skin. "Why do you fight me, Lindsay? Listen to your body, to your racing heart."

With a shuddering explosion of desire she felt his hand cup the smooth fullness of her breast, taunting, coaxing, until she was breathless from desire.

"Please, no!" she sobbed, fighting desperately to hang on to some measure of sanity.

"Why not?" he answered. Through the moonlight he looked down on her creamy nakedness. "You're a beautiful woman," he told her softly, his voice caressing, intoxicating. "Don't deny that you want this as much as I do."

He pressed closer, his strong hands pulling her hips against his, his need urgent, until, of its own accord, her body writhed in exquisite anguish beneath him. To the deepest fiber of her soul, Lindsay wanted to scream yes to his demands. Slowly, tormentingly, his muscular frame still molded to hers, he eased her back against the bench, and to her shame her hips arched to press even tighter against his firm body.

"That's better," he murmured, continuing his insidious invasion of her body. Lindsay moaned as a knee moved between her legs. "That's right, relax," he told her, his whisper smooth as velvet in her ear. "As long as we're thrown together like this why shouldn't we enjoy each other? I know the kind of life you and Alex led." At the slight stiffening of her body, he went on quickly, persuasively, "Relax, Lindsay."

For a spellbinding moment, Lindsay felt as if she was suspended, held captive between the two worlds of desire and reality, as Philip's words sank into her muddled consciousness, then, with a strength born of fury, she lurched sideways, twisting her body until she was free of his imprisoning arms. Clutching her disordered clothing about her naked breasts, she pulled away from the bench.

"How dare you!" she cried, her body, so recently fired by desire, shaking now with unrepressed rage.

"And how dare you be a hypocrite," Philip retorted, his breath still short, his eyes gleaming pools in the moonlight. His body was taut as he stood, his expression contemptuous. "That was a damn sudden change of heart, wouldn't you say? It's a good deal too late now for your sweet little Miss Innocence act. Don't forget, I knew your husband very well."

"And because of that you've decided to condemn me," Lindsay threw back. "Just like that. No trial, no judge, no jury."

"There's no need for judgments. I know what sort of woman Alex would marry." Philip's dark eyes roamed flagrantly over her disheveled figure, causing Lindsay's cheeks to flame beneath the soft glow of moonlight. Unconsciously, she drew her dress tighter across her bosom.

"You're the most arrogant, overbearing man I've ever met!" Lindsay trembled in rage, wanting nothing so desperately as to wipe the smug look off his handsome face. "No wonder Alex wanted to forget New Zealand. You must have made his life hell!"

Philip took a step toward her, and Lindsay instinctively shrank back at the look of smoldering fury in his dark eyes. His strong hands clenched her so roughly by the shoulders that she gave a little cry of surprise.

"You have no idea what you're talking about," he told her, his face ominous. Then, with a sudden shake, he released her, causing Lindsay to stagger back a step or two to retain her balance. "No one's forcing you to stay at Kia Ora," he reminded her sharply. "On the contrary, you're free to leave anytime you like. Just like Alex did."

With a final, mocking nod, he dismissed her, seemingly disdainful now of her nudity. "You talk a good fight, Lindsay," he said, moving toward the house. "But you've got a hell of a long way to go before you prove you've got what it takes to be a vintner."

5

Despite her anger—or was it really her frustration, Lindsay wondered—she was soon asleep, claimed by the exhaustion of unaccustomed labor and lack of rest the night before. But though her body seemed almost drugged with fatigue, her mind rebelliously refused her peace and Lindsay's dreams were far from tranquil.

She and Alex were at a frenzied round of parties and, as usual, her husband was in the thick of things, drinking heavily, talking too loudly and making passes at every pretty woman. Disgusted, Lindsay tried to leave, but rough hands pulled her back, forcing her to dance, to participate in the merrymaking. Miserably, she looked around for a way to escape, but blurred faces closed in around her, blocking her way. And then one face stood out from the rest, dark, tauntingly handsome, with striking blue eyes, and Lindsay's heart lurched.

"Philip," she tried to call. "Help me—" but the words wouldn't form, had no substance. And the dark form merely mocked her as it turned and walked out of the room, leaving her behind.

She ran after him, crying, but a door swung closed in her way, and she was locked in. Frantically she pounded on it with her fists—helpless as she watched the form fade away—

Lindsay was jerked out of her dream by the sound of very real hands knocking on her bedroom door. She blinked in confusion at the sunlight light pouring through the curtains she had been too tired to draw the night before. Squinting, she saw that her small electric alarm clock read six-thirty.

"Miss Lindsay," an urgent voice called. "Are you awake?"

Lindsay rose and grabbed the robe tossed carelessly at the foot of her bed, throwing it over her bare shoulders.

"I'm coming," she said thickly, moving to open the door. She found Inia standing in the hall, her expression so worried that Lindsay's last vestiges of sleep were quickly dispelled. "What's the matter?"

"Have you seen Kiri?" Inia asked anxiously.

Lindsay pushed some unruly strands of blond hair from her eyes and looked at the housekeeper in alarm. "Not since last night. Why? Isn't she in her room?"

Inia looked beside herself. "No. And she didn't sleep there last night."

Lindsay motioned for the housekeeper to come in while she tried to come up with a plausible explanation for the girl's absence. "Maybe she spent the night at a friend's house," she suggested hopefully.

The housekeeper shook her head. "She wouldn't do that without telling me first. She knows how I worry." Inia sank into a chair, and Lindsay could hardly believe the transformation in the lovable despot who ruled the Macek household with an iron hand. "Besides, all her clothes are missing," Inia went on. "She wouldn't need that many just for one night. I was hopin' she might have confided in you."

Lindsay shook her tousled head. "I haven't actually talked to Kiri since early yesterday morning."

"And she didn't say anythin'—about leavin' like this, I mean?"

"No—" Lindsay evaded, reluctant to break a confidence, yet anxious to do all she could to help Inia. But it was not necessary to go on. Inia correctly interpreted her hesitation.

"She told you about Michael, didn't she? And that I want her to forget all that nonsense about being a model."

Lindsay nodded mutely, remembering that part of her advice to the girl had been to do what she thought best. It had never occurred to her that Kiri might run away.

"Well, the girl's makin' a fool of herself," Inia said bitterly, sounding much more like her old self. "It isn't every day a nice, hardworkin' boy like Michael comes along. She should grab him before someone smarter does."

Lindsay wondered how, or even *if*, she should attempt to explain the girl's feelings. "Very often young people have to find these things out for themselves," she ventured.

"And ruin their lives in the process," Inia snorted. The older woman heaved her heavy frame laboriously out of the chair. "I didn't mean to unburden on you like this," she said by way of apology. "But I can't help worryin'. I thought that girl had more sense."

An hour later they found the note. It had been left

carelessly taped to a cupboard in the kitchen, and sometime during the night it must have fallen to the floor to be lost under the table. Actually, Lindsay was the one to make the discovery when her foot brushed against the paper at breakfast. The note was short, and, Lindsay thought when she saw the hastily scrawled words, pathetically dramatic.

Mama,
I'm leaving Kia Ora because I have to follow my dream. I won't tell you where I'm going because I know you'll try to bring me back. Don't worry about me, Mama, I promise I'll be all right.
Please tell Michael I'm sorry it had to be this way, but I know he wouldn't want a wife who was unfulfilled.

Love, Kiri

Inia's response was heartrending. Her normally cheerful face tensed into a mask of disapproval and hurt, and Lindsay experienced a niggling feeling of complicity. She couldn't help wondering how instrumental she had been in the girl's running away. Although she hadn't actually counseled Kiri to leave Kia Ora, she had sympathized with her problem and had even encouraged her to do her own thing. Regretfully, she remembered advising the girl that it was better to make a mistake than not to try at all. Then, with a sigh, Lindsay realized that self-recrimination at this point was useless. The girl was legally of age and she was gone. They would simply have to trust to Kiri's ability to make it on her own and hope that she contacted them soon.

Lindsay did not see Philip until shortly after breakfast when they crossed paths as she made her way to the winery. His cool eyes boldly appraised her tight-fitting work jeans and long-sleeved cotton shirt, but he gave no more than a barely perceptible nod as he passed. His frosty demeanor did nothing to cool her still smoldering anger toward him, nor did she feel inclined to discuss Kiri's disappearance. Then, as she joined Rudy to sterilize the aging tanks, she wondered if Philip even knew of the girl's flight. But of course he would know, she told herself shortly. Philip Macek would always be aware of everything that happened at Kia Ora.

She and Rudy finished sterilizing the last tank by mid-afternoon. With a broad grin, he led her through Kia Ora's public gift shop and down a flight of stone stairs to a series of small, dimly lit rooms beneath. They walked past row upon row of racks filled with wine, stored at just the right angle for optimum preservation, and into a well-lit larger room lined on three walls with aging casks. Although one or two customers browsed in the shop above, the tasting room was deserted.

"The last tour was at two o'clock this afternoon," announced the Irishman brightly, "so we can get on with this undisturbed."

With obvious relish, Rudy moved to the center of the room where an oversized oak table was covered by a clean, white cloth. On it was a long line of upright glasses and several small bowls containing pieces of bread and dry crackers, which Rudy explained were to refresh the palate between wines. Nearby, two sinks were attached to the fourth wall where the cellarmaster told her they would spit out the wine after they had completed their tests.

"If you don't spit it out you'll have the devil's own time tellin' even a white wine from a red after a few swigs. But when we're through with followin' the rules, we'll pay some attention to the swallowin' part," he said with a wink.

The little cellarmaster carefully laid out several glasses in front of her, then cleared his throat, as if he were about to deliver an important lecture.

"Now, you understand wine tastin' is serious business, lass," he told her, his pale blue eyes twinkling in his broad, red face. "It's a true art and must be given the undivided attention it deserves."

He plunged an instrument resembling a large-scale pipette into the bunghole of a cask, and Lindsay watched as a clear white fluid filled the vessel. Then, using his thumb as a plug, Rudy gradually released the wine directly into one of the glasses. Repeating the procedure, he handed a second glass to Lindsay.

"Here, lass," he said softly. "Now, let the wine talk to you."

Following the cellarmaster's example, Lindsay twirled the wine around the glass vigorously to aerate it before sniffing it over the rim. Then, slowly, still watching him closely, she sipped a small quantity and let it run over the top and sides of her tongue and palate before spitting the liquid out into the sink.

"Good," Rudy pronounced. "Now ask yourself, 'Is this wine good or bad?' When you can answer that you must ask, 'Do I like this wine?'"

Lindsay smiled, then laughed outright at Rudy's look of mock censure. "It's good, Rudy," she said, "and I like it. But I could never tell you why."

The cellarmaster tried to look exasperated but merely succeeded in looking comical. "Ah, lass," he sighed. "I'm afraid we've a ways to go before you're a true *vigneron*." His blue eyes sparkled. "But then, learnin's half the fun now, isn't it?"

If the learning was fun, Rudy's method of wine tasting was also slightly intoxicating, and Lindsay felt distinctly lightheaded as she walked back to the house half an hour later. As she approached the veranda, she was brought up short by a creamy white convertible parked to the side of the garden. Lindsay wondered who was visiting Kia Ora. Then she remembered: it must be Sara Warner. With all the shock and confusion over Kiri and the subsequent wine tasting she had forgotten that the actress was coming today. And now, despite all her resolutions, her heart sank at the sight of the sleek sports car.

Lindsay made her way into the house through the kitchen, hoping she might avoid seeing the beautiful Miss Warner. But as she crossed the hallway toward the stairs she met Philip and the actress, who were descending hand in hand from the upper floor. Illogically, Lindsay felt a flush of indignation as she surmised where they had been. Was Philip in the habit of entertaining beautiful young women in his bedroom, she wondered? For Stephanie's sake, she hoped not.

"Hello, Lindsay," Sara said, her clear, green eyes sweeping over Lindsay's distinctly untidy work clothes. "I hear you're becoming quite the vintner."

Lindsay tried to return the actress's smile but was afraid her expression looked stiff and constrained by comparison. Today Sara was wearing her auburn hair more casually than the night of the play; the shoulder-length locks were feathered back from her smooth, oval face into a layered, windswept style. Her sheer, pale green dress was simple, yet extremely feminine, and Lindsay was acutely conscious of her own faded blue jeans and old plaid cotton shirt.

"Let's say I'm doing my best to learn," Lindsay answered quietly. She was aware of the sardonic smile playing at the corners of Philip's mouth. Did he find this meeting so amusing? she asked herself angrily. Well, she would not allow him to think she was jealous. With her brightest smile, she turned to the actress. "I thoroughly enjoyed your performance the other night, Miss Warner," she told her sincerely. "I hope the play is running well."

"Please call me Sara." The actress smiled. "And yes, the play is doing very well, thank you. We may even have to extend it another week if the house continues to sell out." Sara Warner paused for a moment as she drew a well-manicured hand through Philip's arm. "Perhaps if you're still here you could come see us again," she said.

Lindsay glanced quickly at Philip. How much had he told the actress of her plans? Evidently, he had not mentioned her impromptu decision to stay on at the vineyard.

"It's quite likely I'll be here for some time," Lindsay answered, and was secretly pleased to see the shadow which crossed the lovely face. Then she was instantly contrite. What right did she have to intrude on Sara Warner's happiness? It was obvious she loved Philip; she had known him since they were children. Lindsay was the interloper. All things considered, she wondered if she would be as gracious if she were in the actress's position.

"I'm sure Philip must appreciate your help," Sara said, although Lindsay could see that her glance at the vintner was questioning. Still, the actress retained her smile as she turned back to Lindsay. "And I hope Philip's told you about the little party we're giving my father the day after tomorrow in honor of his birthday," she went on. "It's nothing too formal, but I'd really like you to come."

Lindsay glanced at Philip and wondered why he had said nothing to her about a party. Was he afraid she and the actress might become too friendly? If that was the case he needn't have worried, because Lindsay was certain that Sara's invitation was strictly a matter of form. After all, it would be awkward to invite Philip and not his cousin from America.

"Thanks, Sara," Lindsay said, trying very hard to return the actress's smile, "but I'm afraid I've already made plans for that night." Did she imagine that Sara's hold on Philip's arm tightened imperceptibly? Certainly the actress's smile seemed warmer now. "It was very nice of you to ask me, though," she finished hurriedly. Feeling suddenly very much the outsider, Lindsay moved toward the stairs.

"Please excuse me," she said hastily, "but I'm really tired from this morning. I thought I'd take a nap before dinner."

Hardly waiting for their approval, Lindsay fled up the stairs, anxious only to be alone in her room, to sort out her bewildering, conflicting feelings. Why had the sight of the actress thrown her into such turmoil? Surely Philip was entitled to his private life. She had no claim, indeed *wanted* no claim on his affections. Still, the thought of Philip and the gorgeous Sara Warner alone in his bedroom was unnerving, especially after his behavior with her in the garden last night. How could he make love to her one minute and invite the beautiful actress to his bedroom the next?

The answer was so obvious that Lindsay's blood ran cold. She meant absolutely nothing to him, of course. She was merely a pleasant diversion, a challenging conquest conveniently housed under his own roof. *Let's face it*, she told herself bluntly, *I'm just a stopgap between his visits with Sara Warner*. Was it this sort of callous behavior which had driven Stephanie's mother to suicide?

This thought, coupled with the wine she had consumed, made Lindsay's head ache. Searching the bathroom cabinet she found two aspirin and, throwing off her soiled clothes, sank gratefully onto the comfortable bed. How could she let Philip use her like this? And how could she face Sara Warner knowing how close she had come to giving herself completely to the man the actress loved? Lindsay stared dry eyed at the delicate bouquets of violets dotting the cheerful wallpaper. Worst of all, how could she reconcile her determination to stay at Kia Ora with her longing for this man who threatened the very core of her self-respect?

Lindsay was startled by a knock at the door, and a moment later Inia peered into the room. Raising her head, Lindsay realized she had been sleeping for over two hours.

"You're wanted on the phone," the housekeeper told her. "It's Mr. Nicholson from the theater."

Lindsay threw on her clothes and hurried downstairs, taking the call in the kitchen, well away from the sounds of laughter emanating from the parlor.

"I thought we might go to dinner, if you're free," the actor said after she picked up the receiver. "There's no performance tonight, and I am in dire need of another dose of adoration. Would you consent to accompany me to a delightful little hideaway which just happens to have the finest seafood on North Island?"

Lindsay laughed even as she hesitated. Although she'd known that the actor would call sooner or later, she hadn't yet decided on her response. And the way she felt now, the last thing she wanted to do was socialize. Then, at an especially explosive gale of merriment from the other room, she suddenly made her decision. "I'd love to go, Roger," she told him quickly. "Getting out is just what I need right now."

"*Magnífico!*" came the pleased reply from the other end of the line. "I'll pick you up at seven."

Back in her room, Lindsay showered and dressed carefully, choosing a simply cut turquoise blue dress that she knew complemented her tawny hair and warm brown eyes. Adjusting the scooped neckline over her generous bosom, Lindsay applied slightly more makeup than usual, then brushed her long blond hair until it shone with golden highlights. A few minutes with the curling iron coaxed the silken locks to fall in soft waves around her face. Gold loop earrings and a delicate chainlink necklace came next, then a fleeting spray of her favorite scent, and her preparations were complete. She reached for a light wrap and made her way downstairs, determined to wait for Roger on the porch.

"Where are you going?" a low voice said, forcing her to stop just short of the front door.

Turning, Lindsay found Philip standing outside the parlor door, holding a cocktail glass in his hand. Behind him, she could see Sara Warner curled comfortably on the couch, watching them curiously.

"Roger Nicolson and I are going to dinner," Lindsay replied shortly, certain that her social life could be of no consequence to him while the lovely actress was present.

"I see." His dusky blue eyes roamed boldly over her outfit, coming to rest on the soft fullness beneath the scooped neck of her dress. "You certainly dressed for the occasion."

Lindsay's cheeks flushed under his scrutiny. "Did you expect me to wear jeans and a sweat shirt?" She reached a hand out for the door, desperate to be away from him and the beautiful woman waiting for him on the couch. "I have to go now," she murmured, and hurried outside to wait for Roger's arrival away from Philip's penetrating eyes.

She and Roger dined at a delightful little restaurant

overlooking Waitemata Harbour. The seafood, as promised, was excellent, and Lindsay soon found herself relaxing, even laughing, as Roger related vignettes of past and present adventures in his theatrical career. The actor was a delightful companion and for a short while, at least, she was able to forget Philip Macek and the beautiful Sara Warner as she enjoyed after-dinner drinks and dancing at the small Auckland nightclub.

Then, on the way home, it happened. Roger had chosen to drive his vintage MG sedan back to the vineyard via a scenic, if circuitous, route that took them by Cox Bay. There they were startled by an ominous thump under the hood and the almost immediate red flash of the generator light.

"Damn!" Roger exclaimed, pulling the MG over to the side of the road.

"Do you think it's serious?" Lindsay asked nervously, noting by her wristwatch that it was close to one o'clock.

"With this archaic vehicle it is *always* serious," he said, getting out of the sedan. "My cars never manage a moderate illness. With them it's invariably terminal."

Gingerly, the actor lifted the hood and, with the aid of a flashlight, poked about for a minute or two before diagnosing the difficulty.

"The fan belt appears to be broken," he said, finally raising his head from under the hood and wiping his hands on a handkerchief. "In fact, I think we could accurately describe it as pulverized."

"Does that mean we're stuck?"

"It would be impossible to be any more stuck, my dear Lindsay. I'm afraid I'll have to walk to a telephone."

"You're not going to leave me here," Lindsay objected. "I'll go with you."

Looking at her thin high-heeled shoes, Roger shook his head. "You'll break your pretty neck," he pronounced. "Or at the very least get a devilish bunch of blisters. The nearest town is a good three kilometers down the road."

Lindsay peered into the darkness ahead, then drew her thin wrap closer to ward off the increasingly chill night air. Resolutely, she grabbed her purse off the seat and slammed the car door shut behind her.

"I'm going," she told him firmly. "Anything's better than sitting here alone waiting."

It was nearly four o'clock before the taxi Roger finally summoned from a deserted service station phonebox deposited them at the vineyard.

"My profound regrets that the evening turned out so dismally," he told her at the door. "Unfortunately, my calling is not always synonymous with a regular paycheck or I would have terminated my association with that disreputable MG long before this."

Lindsay smiled up at the actor, sensitive to the real embarrassment behind the blithe words. "It's all right, really," she assured him. "I've always wanted to see New Zealand by moonlight."

"Spoken like a real trooper," he laughed. Then, more seriously, "And a very beautiful one, at that."

Gently, the actor drew her into his arms and kissed her lightly on the forehead, then more deliberately on the lips; it was a tender, sensitive embrace. "I'd like to see you again—very soon," the actor whispered when they finally parted. "I promise to have the MG working smooth as a top."

"I'd like that," Lindsay answered. She smiled up at him, so uncharacteristically intent in the moonlight. "I had a wonderful time, Roger, really. In spite of the car. Thank you." Then, reaching up, she planted a light kiss on his cheek before slipping through the door and into the house.

Reluctant to make any unnecessary noise, Lindsay stood for a moment letting her eyes get used to the dark before proceeding to the stairs. The hallway was so quiet that she gave a little scream as a strong arm reached out and grabbed her by the waist. At the same moment, the hall light switched on.

"That was a touching scene out there," Philip told her, his low tone dripping sarcasm. "You and Roger seem to have become very close friends."

"We had an enjoyable evening," she told him stiffly. "But I'm tired now, so if you'll let me—"

"Go to bed?" Philip broke in. "You mean you haven't been there already? It's after four, you know. Or have you been too busy to notice?"

Philip's words stung. "Not that it's any of your business, but we had car problems."

"How original," Philip retorted, tightening his hold on her waist. "A clever young woman like you should be more creative."

"It happens to be the truth," she snapped, then realized the futility of further reasoning. "But I'm sure you'll believe what you want. You always do," she added shortly. "Now, will you please let me go? You're hurting me."

With a quick movement, Philip released her, and Lindsay almost stumbled on feet already aching and bruised by the long trek along the coast. The look he gave her was withering, and Lindsay's heart sank despite her resolutions.

"I'll be happy to release you, *Mrs. Macek*," he said, his voice dagger sharp in Lindsay's heart. "I wouldn't want to trespass on another man's property." He seemed to lose interest as he turned for the stairs.

"Oh, by the way," he threw back. "We're going to Auckland tomorrow morning to see the enologist."

At Lindsay's astonished look he continued, "You *are* interested in the workings of the vineyard, aren't you? At least that's what you keep telling me."

"If it concerns Kia Ora, then of course I'm interested," she threw back at him.

"Good. Then I'll see you at nine sharp." He smiled at her with hateful complacency. "Good night, Lindsay. Pleasant dreams."

6

They were halfway to Auckland when Lindsay discovered she was in love with Philip, had in all likelihood started loving him that day on the beach when his lips first found hers. The realization was at once startling and obvious, although how it came about was a mystery. Certainly she hadn't set out to fall in love, especially with Philip Macek, nor had she been consciously aware of it happening. Of course, with the advantage of hindsight she could see that there had been any number of warning signs: her joy that morning on Mount Eden when they'd shared the New Zealand sunrise, the longing she'd felt the other night in the garden when every part of her cried out for the total merging of their bodies and, of course, yesterday, her uneasiness at Sara Warner's visit.

Even a child would have recognized the biting pangs of the jealousy she'd felt when the actress arrived at Kia Ora, the almost physical pain of watching Sara and Philip share a world forever closed to her. Then, last night, when Roger had taken her in his arms, the final doubts had been removed. With all her heart she had wanted to respond to the actor's embrace, but she'd felt nothing more than a platonic warmth that could in no way compare with the frightening desire she experienced with Philip.

Lindsay leaned back against the soft white seat, watching as Philip easily guided the Aston Martin through the lovely New Zealand countryside. She looked covertly at his profile: the strong, almost Roman nose, the disturbing cobalt-blue eyes, and, worst of all, that devilishly sensuous mouth. Why did she have such an unerring knack for falling in love with men who could only hurt her?

Lindsay closed her eyes tightly, blocking him from her field of vision. For the worst of it was, of course, that Philip did not return her love, took no effort, in fact, to conceal his resentment toward her. Lindsay knew only too well that she was merely a physical distraction to him, one that would be quickly forgotten in Sara Warner's arms. Had it been this way for Stephanie's mother, Lindsay wondered? Had she, too, been unable to cope with the vintner's casual disregard for love?

The thought only strengthened Lindsay's resolve. Under no circumstances must Philip ever suspect her true feelings. Her only defense against this madness was to maintain a completely businesslike facade. She must think only of Kia Ora, not of its disturbing owner.

"Hey, wake up. We'll be there in a few minutes." Philip was looking at her in annoyance. "If you're going to stay out all night you'd better be prepared to pay the price."

Startled, Lindsay sat upright and straightened her

skirt, which had risen to reveal shapely knees. "I wasn't asleep," she said shortly. "Just thinking."

"About Roger, I suppose. I'm surprised you haven't outgrown that sort of mooning."

A retort sprang to Lindsay's lips, but she quickly suppressed it. What did it matter what he thought? In fact, it might simplify matters if he assumed she was interested in the actor.

"You haven't really explained what sort of work the enologist is doing for Kia Ora," Lindsay said, ignoring his remark.

"Hansen monitors all our wine. He checks for obvious strengths and weaknesses, as well as for more subtle levels of acidity and sweetness. Right now, he's running a series of tests on the varietals."

"And how does it look? Will they be a success?"

"Unfortunately, it's impossible to tell from a test tube. All Hansen can do is to eliminate the more obvious pitfalls. The human palate is still the only real test of excellence." He threw her a contemptuous look. "But don't lose heart, we could still fail. Then I'd be forced to agree to the sale of Kia Ora. You may be a wealthy woman yet."

Richard Hansen's modern, well-equipped offices were located just off Victoria Park. The enologist was surprisingly young, no more than twenty-eight or -nine, and very friendly. When Lindsay commented on his amazing amount of lab equipment, he enthusi-astically launched into an explanation of his work.

"Enological research covers a wide range of projects," he said with obvious pride. "Science is exerting increasing influence on which vines are planted, how they are planted and where, as well as what should be done during and after the harvest."

"It sounds a lot like our hybrid corn experiments back home," Lindsay told him with interest. "Science has become very important on the farm, too."

Richard Hansen's face lit. "I didn't know you were a farm girl, Mrs. Macek," he exclaimed happily.

"Lindsay comes from Iowa," Philip said, his dark blue eyes searching hers thoughtfully. "Although I must admit I had no idea she was a farmer."

"But I'm not—I mean, I haven't been in a long time," Lindsay answered, flustered that her casual remark had been taken so seriously. "I was raised on a farm just outside of Ames. We grew some soybeans, but our major crop was corn."

Richard rubbed his hands in delight. "But that's wonderful," he said. "My aunt and uncle grow corn in Kansas." He turned to Lindsay eagerly. "Tell me, what kind of corn do you grow?"

"Dent corn," Lindsay answered. "Yellow dent."

"And the hybrid?"

"Pioneer 33-82," she said, smiling. "And, before you ask, the average yield is about 125 bushels per acre."

"Feed corn?"

"Some, yes. Iowa's full of hog farms, you know. But we also sold to companies who extract the fructose for commercial use."

"Good," Richard proclaimed. "Really very good." He grinned broadly. "You're right, you know. There are any number of similarities between my work and the hybrid research that's going on. You must feel right at home on the vineyard."

Lindsay nodded, but her meaningful smile was reserved for Philip. "Yes, I'm very attached to Kia Ora."

*   *   *

"Why didn't you tell me you were raised on a farm?" Philip asked the minute they were back at the car.

Enjoying his rare discomposure, she shrugged off-handedly. "You never asked."

He was eyeing her skeptically. "Yet you left Iowa to move to Hollywood with Alex."

Lindsay tilted her face so she could look directly into his cobalt eyes. "I loved the farm, Philip," she said pointedly, "and I love California. They're both special to me, just as Kia Ora is. Is that so difficult to understand?"

Philip shook his dark head. "No, I guess not. But you sure as hell are."

With a quick flip of his wrist, Philip turned the key in the ignition, and the high-powered car sprang to life. Pulling out into traffic, Philip drove for several blocks before parking in front of a row of quaint, Victorian-style structures.

"Why are we stopping here?" Lindsay asked.

Philip gave a throaty chuckle. "I don't know. Do I have to have a reason? It just seems a shame to go directly back to the vineyard." He walked around to her side of the car and threw open the door. "Besides," he grinned, "this seems like a good day for surprises."

As she took his hand for balance, Lindsay marveled at the unusual sparkle of laughter in his dark eyes. She realized, suddenly, how infrequently Philip smiled, how his face much more frequently reflected the strain of running the vineyard, of the calculated risk he had taken that might result in the loss of a hundred-year-old heritage. She decided she much preferred him this way.

"This is historic Parnell," he told her, "one of

Auckland's oldest districts." He indicated the carefully refurbished 19th-century structures. "As a boy I loved to wander around these old buildings."

Lindsay had a sudden, irrepressible desire to have known Philip as a child. What had he been like? Somehow, she couldn't imagine him as anything other than the confident, self-assured man he was now.

"Come on," he prompted, linking her arm in his. "I have a sudden urge to be frivolous today."

For more than an hour they strolled through the complex of Victorian structures, which, despite the many shops, food stores, art galleries and restaurants, still gave a delightful feeling of cohesive, small-town charm. Then, at the top of a hill overlooking the district, they explored the simple Gothic, Anglican church buildings, which Philip explained had been built by Bishop Selwyn, a missionary of the mid-1800s. Finally, they sipped hot, strong tea and shared sandwiches in Parnell Rose Gardens, the beautiful blooms surrounding them with a lush blanket of red, yellow, pink and white.

"It's been a wonderful morning," Lindsay sighed, breathing in the rich fragrance of the roses. She had to admit she was enjoying the unexpected truce which had settled, unspoken, between them. Even though she knew it couldn't last, Lindsay was powerless to resist sharing the stolen moments before returning to a harsher reality.

Philip grinned and Lindsay was once again struck by the way his face lit up.

"It has been great," he laughed. "Why is it that playing hooky is so damn much fun? It's almost a shame to go back to work." He looked at her quizzically for a moment, then rose suddenly from the bench where they had been eating. "Come on," he said, abruptly, taking Lindsay firmly by the hand. "We might as well waste the whole day while we're at it."

Back in the car, Philip turned the Aston Martin northeast toward Hauraki Gulf, away from Henderson.

"Where are we going?" she asked as he parked at the Ferry Building.

"You'll see." Philip wore a look of wry amusement as he led her onto a public launch. Although the vessel was nearly full, they were able to find good seats in the aft section of the boat.

The trip through the Tamaki Strait and out into Hauraki Gulf was beautiful; the sea was calm and clear, the many islands dotting the coast welcome oases of golden sand and lush green trees.

"That's Motuihe Island," Philip said when they were about an hour out of Auckland. "And that big island over there is Waiheke, the largest in the gulf. There are some farms sprinkled around the island, but mainly it's a retirement mecca." Philip's smile was playful. "Maybe because the fishing's so good."

Lindsay watched the islands recede as the launch continued on into the gulf. She found the ride heady, almost as intoxicating as the wine she had sampled the day before. The sky enclosed them in a glorious azure-blue umbrella while the sun showered them with a tingling rainfall of warmth. But it was Philip, his body alive and vibrant beside her, his scent clean and profoundly masculine, who inebriated her senses and terrified her better judgment. She felt little prickles of fire as his fingers traced lazy patterns on her arm, his touch undoing all her resolutions. Yet despite her misgivings and her sure knowledge of the futility of their relationship, she felt unaccountably secure, ridiculously serene in his arms. With closed eyes, she listened to the gentle hum of the boat's motor as it cut steadily through the water.

They reached Pakatoa Island just as the sun became a blazing ball of flame in the western sky, and for a moment they stood quietly on the dock as it bathed the tropical greenery with an orange-red glow.

"It's breathtaking," Lindsay whispered, enthralled by the vibrant splash of color.

"I thought you'd like it. We have until ten to enjoy the island. That's when the last launch goes back to Auckland."

Taking Lindsay's arm, Philip led her off the dock and onto a sandy beach sprawled at the foot of a slight, bush-covered incline. They followed a winding path into a subtropical paradise of lush green trees and plants, their progress lighted by the glow of electric lamps placed at regular intervals. Soon, they came upon a small white chalet off to the right, then another set a hundred feet or so beyond that to the left.

"Pakatoa Island is a popular honeymoon hideaway," Philip explained with a grin. "There are a number of self-contained chalets and, further on, a hotel and restaurant. The food's pretty good, but the view is spectacular."

Later, as they sat at a picture window in the dining room of the hotel restaurant, Lindsay thought Philip's appraisal of the food was far too modest. The rock lobster was excellent, its flavor distinctive yet delicate, the meat moist and succulent. The braised potatoes and steamed broccoli, unfortunately, received a slightly lower mark, but Lindsay was getting used to the fact that New Zealanders invariably overcook their vegetables. Happily, the green salad was crisp and very fresh and dessert, tiny, sweet-filled pancakes, was absolutely delicious. Of course, the wine was superb, and even Lindsay's inexperienced palate could appreciate the mellow aroma and smooth texture of the Chenin Blanc, which she was proud to see carried the Kia Ora label.

As they ate, Lindsay noticed that the trees and bushes outside the hotel were blowing with increasing vigor, and one tall *nikau* palm brushed urgently against their window. Then, as she watched, the first large droplets of rain pattered onto the pane, rapidly increasing into a downpour that blew onto the window with force.

"What is it?" she asked, noticing that Philip, too, was staring outside.

"A late summer squall," he answered tersely. "Sometimes they hit well into autumn."

Lindsay looked at her watch. It was after nine. "But the launch—"

"Exactly. No boat will venture through these islands during a storm."

The rain now beat a frantic tattoo on the window. Outside, the bushes and red-flowered *pohutukawas* swayed almost perpendicular in the wind.

"Maybe it won't last long," she said hopefully, realizing her voice barely carried over the gale winds now raging across the little island.

Philip shrugged broad shoulders. "Who knows? Sometimes they last ten minutes, sometimes five hours. We'll just have to wait and see."

But by ten o'clock it was obvious the storm was not going to abate.

"Looks like we're stuck," Philip said, and a corner of his mouth twitched as he turned toward the desk. "I'll get us some rooms, then call home and tell them what happened. Fortunately, there are worse places than this to be stranded."

Five minutes laters, however, Lindsay wasn't so sure of their good fortune, as it became apparent that every other visitor in the dining room was also marooned.

"Guess we'll have to share a room," Philip said, grinning lazily.

"But—we can't," Lindsay protested, her heart giving a sudden lurch. "There's no way I'm going to sleep in the same room with you tonight."

Philip nodded pleasantly. "Suit yourself." He looked around the small, old-fashioned lobby. "I hope you won't be too uncomfortable." Without glancing back, he started up the stairs.

Lindsay paused, realizing only too clearly her limited options. Either she could make a fool of herself trying to curl up here in the lobby on one of those ridiculous straight-backed Victorian chairs, or she could take the chance of sharing a room with the man she loved. Lindsay stifled a shiver of apprehension. Was it Philip she didn't trust or herself? Then, at a curious look from the large, austere woman behind the desk, Lindsay made her decision and hurried up the stairs after Philip's tall figure.

The room was small but scrupulously clean, and, in typical New Zealand fashion, had a small sink and mirror in one corner. The bath, she knew, would be down the hall to be shared with other guests on that floor. The most outstanding feature, although Lindsay realized she was probably oversensitive, was the large double bed, which seemed, in some disturbing way, to fill the room.

Philip was already removing his jacket when Lindsay came in, and his dark eyes seemed to read her thoughts with wry amusement.

"You look as if you're afraid I'm going to ravish you," he said, pulling the shirttail out of his slacks.

Lindsay carelessly threw her handbag onto a chair, wishing only that her turbulent emotions matched the outward calm she had chosen to adopt. "Don't be ridiculous," she said lightly. "I have no intention of being ravished."

She watched as he unbuttoned, then peeled off the soft blue shirt, revealing the expanse of thick crisp dark hair underneath. When she went on, she was annoyed to find that her voice was not as controlled as she would have liked. "We're both adults. I'm sure we can share a room for one night without imagining nonexistent complications."

Philip grinned, his handsome face now entirely too full of mischief. "Maybe you can, but my imagination can come up with all sorts of delightful complications."

Lindsay could not control the quickened beat of her pulse at the all too suggestive expression on Philip's face. Then, when he began to unzip his slacks, she hastily grabbed her purse and moved back to the door.

"I think I'll have a quick shower before turning in," she said without looking back. "Don't wait up for me. I know you must be tired."

"So are you," came the disturbing voice from behind her. "After all it's because of you that I lost so much sleep last night, remember?" He chuckled lightly. "Hurry back."

But Lindsay did not hurry. She took a leisurely shower, allowing the hot water to flow at full force over her shoulders and back until her skin tingled. Then, after vigorously toweling herself dry, she carefully washed off her makeup at the sink, staring in dismay at the glowing face that peered back at her from the mirror. She shouldn't be radiant, she told herself angrily, releasing her frustration by brushing furiously at her long hair. How could she possibly remain strong when her body betrayed her at every turn?

It was a full hour before Lindsay returned to the room, and she breathed a deep sigh of relief when she saw that the light was out. Closing the door with infinite care, she used the diffused moonlight that filtered through the curtained window to tiptoe to the overstuffed chair in the corner. Then, holding still as a statue, she listened to the slow, even breathing coming from the bed. The storm had finally subsided, and the island was so quiet that Lindsay imagined she could hear her own heartbeat as she waited. After a full minute she was finally satisfied that he was asleep, then immediately wondered at the utter disappointment she felt at this discovery. Furious at her subversive emotions, Lindsay threw herself down on the chair where she had already planned to spend the night. It was the only safe way she could think of to get through the ordeal.

"You aren't really going to spend the night there, are you?"

Lindsay started as the unexpected words cut through the dark room. "I thought you were asleep," she said, disconcerted.

"That's obvious. You were gone so long I thought maybe you'd decided to swim back to Auckland."

"I didn't realize you were timing me," she replied stiffly. "I enjoyed a nice warm shower."

Philip chuckled softly in the darkness. "Good. Now, why don't you come over here and enjoy a nice warm bed?"

"No, thank you," Lindsay replied, her voice unnaturally constricted. "As a matter of fact, I'm not very tired. I think I'll just sit here for a while and enjoy the evening."

"You're going to be cold," he warned, and Lindsay found the amused lilt to his voice annoying.

"I'm quite comfortable," she retorted, and settled herself in the slightly lumpy chair.

"But it's much more cozy over here," he teased, the humor in his tone unmistakable now.

"I'm just fine, thank you," Lindsay said sharply, leaving no doubt that the subject was closed.

"Have it your way," he said with a yawn. "See you in the morning."

Lindsay heard the old bed creak as Philip turned over and then the room was silent again, too silent. For a moment, she felt an illogical regret that he had not continued the argument, that he hadn't come up with some irrefutable reason why she should join him in the bed. Then, with a sigh, she leaned back in the chair, allowing her long hair to fan freely about her face. Why should she be disappointed that he was in the bed and she was on the chair? After all, that was what she wanted, what she had planned. But even as she berated herself, she wondered why the argument sounded so unconvincing.

For the first hour, she was fairly comfortable. From the chair she could see the outlines of the tall palm trees outside, their upper leaves barely moving now in the slight breeze which fanned the island. It was almost unbelievable that they had shuddered with such force only a few hours ago. She breathed deeply of the fragrant night air, so fresh now from the recent rain and watched the flicker of several bright stars that illuminated the New Zealand sky. How very peaceful, she thought lazily. It really was a beautiful little island. So tranquil and serene—

Lindsay awoke with a start, conscious of being thoroughly chilled. Not only was she shivering, but it also seemed as if every bone in her body ached from her cramped position in the chair. Stretching out protesting limbs, she saw by the luminous dial on her watch that it was just after 1:00 A.M. She had hardly been asleep one hour. But during that time, the comfortable breeze flowing from the open window had grown chill and she was shivering so badly her teeth chattered. Lindsay clutched her sweater, the only wrap she had thought to take along that morning, more closely about her, but the effort was futile. She was still freezing.

Lindsay looked longingly at the inviting bed. It hardly seemed fair that Philip should be so warm and comfortable while she suffered on the chair. Surely he ought to have done the gentlemanly thing and offered to let her have the bed. Of course, he *had* offered to share it, she reminded herself caustically. Suddenly, she understood his little game. He knew very well she would freeze in the chair, knew it was just a matter of time until she came begging to be allowed into his bed. Well, his little plan wouldn't work, she determined angrily. She wouldn't let it work. If he had the bed, the least she would have was some covering.

Rising from the chair, Lindsay stole quietly around the bed until she was opposite Philip. Then, finding the end of the blanket, she carefully tugged on a corner until it began to slip gently over his sleeping figure. Suddenly, he stirred, and Lindsay froze until his breathing became even again. Then, as she reached over to slip the edge of the blanket out from under the mattress, a strong hand gripped her wrist.

"So, you decided to join me after all."

Lindsay caught her breath as the fingers held her arm in a steellike grip.

"No—I was just—" Lindsay stopped. How in the world *could* she explain what she was doing?

"Stealing my blanket?" came the mocking reply.

Lindsay shivered, as much from his touch as from

the chill that still gripped her body. "I was cold," she answered lamely.

With one small movement, Philip pulled her down beside him on the bed. His voice was husky, his breath warm and sweet on her cheek. "But I can take care of that much better than a blanket."

Fitting his actions to the words, he drew her against him, sheltering her within his arms. Then, with exquisite tenderness, his lips brushed hers, their teasing softness a slow, maddening torture. His mouth was gentle, and his hand caressed the small of her back as his lips playfully traced kisses over each eye, then moved slowly down to the tip of her slightly upturned nose. With another light brush on her lips, his mouth moved across her cheek, his tongue tracing small circles of fire in her ear, her neck, her hair, his breath warm and unbelievably sensuous. Then, again, his mouth was on hers, his touch light, tantalizing, until, nearly insane with longing, her own lips parted and claimed his with an intensity that threatened to consume them both.

His response was immediate, and his tongue probed her mouth eagerly, searching, exploring, causing dizzying waves of desire to course through her body, leaving her weak with longing. Without conscious thought, Lindsay's hands traveled to the back of his neck, her fingers massaging his tanned skin, pulling him even closer.

Then his lips left her mouth to trail a path of burning little kisses down to the hollow of her throat. Smoothly, his fingers found the back zipper of her dress and slowly eased it down to below the waist. With greater insistency now, he brushed aside the cool cotton until all that protected her was the flimsy material of her lacy bra. Slowly, his mouth moved down her neck, coming to rest on the full swell of her breasts. Unfastening the last constraint, he slipped the straps off her shoulders, exposing pink nipples already taut with desire.

With tantalizing leisure, he captured first one nipple then the other, tormenting them with his teeth, torturing them with slow, maddening circles with his tongue, until they peaked with desire.

"Stop, Philip," she groaned, trying to fight the shivering sensations that were blotting out sanity. But there was no stopping her own impassioned response, and her hands moved shamelessly over his neck and back, delighting in the sensual, hard ripple of his muscles beneath her fingers.

"I've been patient long enough," he whispered, his voice hoarse in her ear. "I want you, Lindsay."

She felt his hands move with new urgency down the soft curves of her body, and the remainder of her clothes quickly gave way to his fiery voyage of exploration until she lay naked beside him. Throwing back the sheet, he pulled her to him. As her straining breasts brushed the soft down of his chest, she realized he, too, was naked beneath the covers, and the discovery only fanned the already raging flame of her desire.

With infinite patience, his fingers continued their probe, tracing the smooth curves of her body, awakening the most sensitive areas until her whole being cried out to be fulfilled. With a little moan, she arched her hips into his, and her hands reached out to caress his naked thighs, to stroke and mold them into hers.

Shuddering at her touch, his lips once again found hers, but gone was the forbearance, the earlier patience, as they claimed possession with a hungry, eager insistence quickly matched by her own. Lindsay's fevered body twisted in delicious agony as she felt the cool, hard contact of his body. Her hands, seemingly powered by a force beyond her control, lost themselves in the wanton discovery of his body, moving where they should not, massaging, caressing, increasing his arousal. With a wrenching shiver, she felt herself sinking, falling into a great abyss from which there could be no escape, from which she had no desire to escape.

"Now, Lindsay," he groaned, and she felt his desperate need, his pounding heart on hers as he repositioned her slightly on the bed, his knees easing her legs apart.

Then, with a magnetism as old as time, they were drawn inexorably together, joined in a searing, consuming fire of longing. She strained upward beneath his thrusting body, as passions too long dormant awakened to his expert touch. With perfectly choreographed harmony, they melded together, his strong, hard form against her soft, yielding flesh, until, with an uncontrolled cry of passion, they were engulfed in a cataclysmic explosion of fulfillment.

7

Sunshine flooded the room, waking Lindsay to a glorious new day. She stretched like a contented kitten, her still naked body tingling with the memory of last night; then, lazily, she turned toward Philip. She was surprised to find him propped up on one elbow silently watching her.

"Good morning, sleepyhead." He grinned.

"How long have you been awake?" she laughed back. "And why are you just lying there staring at me?"

"To answer your first question, for about half an hour, and your second, because you looked so peaceful in your sleep. *And* lovely," he added huskily.

Teasing him, she pretended to roll away.

"You'd better be careful. You can get in trouble talking like that."

"That's the whole idea," he murmured, burying his head in the soft hair at the nape of her neck.

Lindsay's body quivered in response to the hand that ran gently down the soft curve of her body, coming to rest on her naked thigh. Pulling her closer, he moved his head from her neck to the deep ravine between her breasts, then to the rosy nipples, already aroused from his touch.

This time their lovemaking was more leisurely, tantalizingly thorough. Slowly, sensitively, they explored each other's bodies in the streaming sunlight, delighting in their glowing sensuality, allowing the excitement of discovery to build gradually. His lips found hers and took possession with a kiss that was at once tender and demanding. With complete abandon, she responded, and, as their bodies entwined, she felt the ragged beat of his heart as it pressed against her breast.

Then, at the zenith of their longing, they were joined, the merging of two beings into one, fused together as a whole, once again complete. She felt as if they were on a roller coaster, speeding, spiraling, falling with an urgency even more intense than before, until, with wave after wave of overwhelming bliss, they reached the pinnacle. With a cry of utter ecstasy, she shuddered, then subsided, spent, in Philip's arms.

Outside, only the squawks and thrills of the native sea birds broke the silence of the little room as Lindsay lay with her head cradled in the crook of Philip's arm, content, totally fulfilled.

"I'll have to think of some way to thank the weatherman," he whispered at last.

Lindsay turned her head to better look into those extraordinary blue eyes. "For what?"

"Last night's storm, of course." He smiled. "His timing was perfect."

"So you and the weatherman planned all this, did you?" Lindsay laughed. She rolled off the bed and threw her pillow at him, then ducked as his came flying back at her with far more accuracy.

"You rogue," she said, collapsing in peals of laughter as he captured her and pummeled her teasingly with her own pillow this time.

Philip stopped and looked down at her glowing face as he held her pinned beneath him on the bed. Bending his head, he kissed her tenderly on the mouth, then released her with a little push.

"Get away from me, woman," he said, grabbing for his pants. "Any more of that and we'll never get off this island."

They arrived back at Kia Ora in the early afternoon. As the housekeeper greeted them, Lindsay wondered if her happiness gave away their secret. Already the mirror had shown her there was a new glow in her cheeks, an added sparkle in her clear, brown eyes. Surely the truth must be obvious. Her love must shine as a beacon for the world to see.

Her spirits were somewhat dampened when she heard that there was still no word from Kiri. Although she was bustling around as busily as ever, the housekeeper's concern was depressingly apparent in the darkened shadows under her eyes and the lines of worry fanning out from her full, generous mouth.

"I'm sure Kiri is all right," Lindsay told her, wishing she could be certain of her own words. "After all, look who her mother is. She can take care of herself."

Inia smiled, but Lindsay noticed that most of the light had gone out of the warm, dark eyes. Lindsay felt so helpless. If only there was some way to contact the girl and let her know what her absence was doing to her mother. Why didn't she call?

Philip grabbed a quick bite to eat in the kitchen, then bent to brush a fleeting kiss on Lindsay's cheek before hurrying over to the vineyard.

"Until later," he whispered when the housekeeper's back was turned, and Lindsay felt a warm, blissful glow of well-being spread through her body. Never could she remember being this happy, this fulfilled.

Lindsay helped Inia clean up the luncheon dishes, wondering that even the most mundane chore seemed to bring her joy; then she changed into work clothes and went to find the cellarmaster.

"I hear you got a taste of our fickle New Zealand weather last night," Rudy said cheerfully when she met him outside the crushing room. His pale blue eyes twinkled. "Or were you just usin' a little wind and a few drops of rain as an excuse for gettin' away from me, lass? Maybe I've been workin' you too hard."

"A *little* wind," Lindsay gasped, laughing at the Irishman. "If that's a little wind and a few drops of rain I'd hate to see a *real* New Zealand storm."

"Aye, then you'd have a legitimate excuse for stayin' off the job," the little man said with mock seriousness. "Now, if you think you're rested enough, maybe we can get on with it."

Lindsay laughed, but before she could retort he ducked quickly into the aging room.

"What's on for today?" she asked, thinking that this afternoon the row upon row of barrels seemed to have taken on special meaning. As she looked around the room, she was filled with enormous pride that part, at least, of this vast, fruitful countryside was hers, to nurture and cultivate, to enjoy and feel part of. Then, as she brushed her hand along the rough-

111

grained wood of a cask, she realized what made it so meaningful. She was sharing it with the man she loved.

Rudy led her past the aging barrels into a high-ceilinged room beyond. On either side of this second room were two of the largest tanks Lindsay had ever seen.

"We've got two more aging tanks to clean, lass," he said with a twinkle. "Only they're a mite bigger than the ones back there. The men have been workin' all week bottlin' the contents to make room for this year's vintage. And since you and I are about the right size for the job, I waited until you got back to start."

He handed over her customary rubber boots and apron, then hauled a long hose over to one of the tanks. Removing a small, round gate from the front of the huge tank, he placed it on the floor before climbing onto a step just outside the tiny manhole.

"This is the tricky part," he told her with a wink. Leaning forward, he put his head and hands inside the tank, then moved his body in a way that reminded Lindsay of the first half of a swimmer's butterfly stroke.

"It's all a matter of the shoulders," came a muffled voice from inside the tank. "Once your shoulders clear the portal," he went on, matching his actions to the words, "you have to wriggle forward until you can get one of your legs clear of the gate to stand on inside." With some huffing and puffing, Rudy twisted expertly until Lindsay finally saw his lower half disappear inside the tank. In a moment, Rudy's cheerful face peered out at her again from the bunghole.

"That's all there is to it." He grinned. He cocked his impish head to one side. "Are you game to give it a try, lass?"

Lindsay studied the small hole. Rudy had made it look easy enough. At any rate, if she wanted to be a vintner, she'd have to learn all aspects of the business. With a smile of determination, she nodded to the cellarmaster.

"Sure, why not?"

Getting up on the step, Lindsay followed Rudy's example and stuck her head and arms through the opening. Then, looking at the circumference of the tiny hole, which was only inches bigger than her head, she thought it seemed much smaller now than it had when she'd watched the cellarmaster climb in.

"Are you sure I'll fit?" she asked skeptically.

"If I can make it, so can you," the little man answered reasonably.

Thus encouraged, Lindsay bravely squirmed and twisted, trying to remember how Rudy had managed to make it look so simple. Then, just as she finally got her shoulders through the hole, she realized she was stuck.

"Nice view," came a familiar voice from behind her.

Lindsay flushed to the roots of her blond hair as she imagined the "view" Philip must be getting from the outside of the tank.

"Need some help?" continued the voice.

Before she could refuse, two strong hands gripped her by the hips, and with one strong push she was through the hole, assisted by Rudy on the inside. Standing, Lindsay turned to face her benefactor, whose dark, amused eyes were appraising her flushed face through the opening.

"Thank you," she said, trying to regain some dignity despite the makeshift apron and floppy boots. "Although I'm sure I could have made it on my own."

"Undoubtedly. But I couldn't resist lending a helping hand," he added with a playful grin.

Lindsay darted a warning look at him, but he only laughed harder, and she wondered what the little cellarmaster must think of this rather intimate exchange between his employers. But the Irishman looked thoroughly delighted at their banter. Then she realized he would have heard stories of their fight in the aging room the other day. No wonder he looked relieved that they had buried the hatchet. She only hoped he wouldn't guess to what lengths their peacemaking had taken them.

"However, as charming as your derriere may be, that's not the reason I'm here," Philip added, poking his head farther into the opening. He looked at the cellarmaster. "I hear there's been another delay in delivering the harvester. What's the story?"

Rudy shook his wiry head. "The shipment's been held up for some reason or other. They gave me the usual excuses and promised to have it here in a few days. But I wouldn't take any bets on that," he added with uncharacteristic pessimism. "Everytime I talk to them they come up with a different story."

Philip's face was serious. "They'd better get it here on time. I'm counting on that machine to help cover the overflow from the new vines. And we start picking next week."

"Just how important is that machine?" Lindsay asked Rudy after Philip left.

The cellarmaster shrugged muscular shoulders. "We've never really needed one before this. But because of our expansion over the past few years, it's cheaper to use the harvester than pay the additional men to pick."

The little man pulled the hose through the hole in

the tank as he went on, taking pains to explain in his usual patient manner. "You see, a mechanical picker gets the grapes from the vines to the fermentors a lot faster than hand pickin' does. And any time you can do that, it's always better for the wine. Then, too," he admitted, although Lindsay noted a touch of nostalgia in his kindly voice, "a crew of three can machine-pick an acre in a bit less than an hour. Three hand-pickers can cover no more than a sixth of an acre in the same time." He sighed. "There's no doubt about it, lass. The machine's a big savin'."

Rudy finished showing Lindsay the operation. When he was satisfied she understood, he left to snake his way into the other tank. For three hours they worked, thoroughly hosing the tanks, then burning them with sulfur. When they were finally through, Lindsay was more than ready for a break. But squirming out of the hole seemed to be as difficult as getting in had been.

"You just have to reverse everythin'," the cellarmaster laughed, after several minutes of watching her struggle. "First, you stick one leg out and then the other. Then you wiggle back and forth until your waist can bend outside the tank. After that it's easy enough to back out onto the step here."

Lindsay followed his instructions and found, to her relief, that she seemed to have more talent for getting out of the tank then she'd had for getting in.

"That's a good piece of work," the cellarmaster proclaimed after examining her tank carefully. "I think we'll call it a day." He eyed her soberly. "But I'll expect you back here bright and early tomorrow, lass. Storms notwithstandin'."

"Don't worry, Rudy," she replied brightly, although later she would remember the words ruefully.

"All I have planned for tonight is a nice long soak in the tub and a good night's sleep. You work me too hard for anything else."

Lindsay was hardly inside the house when she was met by an exuberant Stephanie leading a little girl of about the same age.

"Lindsay, this is Jenny," the child bubbled. "We've got some really super news!"

"Don't tell me," Lindsay said, joining in the excitement. "It's about the school play. You got the part!"

"We did! We did!" The two little girls jumped up and down with youthful enthusiasm. "And we're going to rehearse together until we know the roles perfectly. Just like you taught me." The child's dark blue eyes were sparkling. "Papa even said Jenny could spend the night, Lindsay. That means we can practice for hours."

"Wait a minute, Stephie," Lindsay laughed. "Too much rehearsal can ruin the performance. You want to retain some spontaneity for opening night."

"Oh, we will," the little girl told her confidently. "We want to be perfect for our opening night. Just like Sara was." The child's wide eyes appealed to Lindsay. "Would you help us, Lindsay? Please? Then we know it will be right."

Despite her fatigue, Lindsay smiled down at the two eager little faces. "Of course I'll help you." She pulled off her apron. "Come on, ladies. There's no time like the present."

"You aren't ready."

Lindsay looked up from the pants she was hemming to find Philip standing at the open door to her bedroom. She had retired there after coaching the girls on their parts again after dinner. Since Philip had excused himself shortly after coffee, she assumed he was busy at the vineyard.

"Ready for what?" she asked in surprise. She noticed he was wearing a dark, well-cut suit and a cream-colored shirt with matching tie of soft maroon and ivory on a dark blue background.

"The party at the Warners', of course," he told her, beginning to look annoyed. "Don't you remember?"

Lindsay's heart sank. Of course—the party, Sara Warner's party. With all that happened on the island she had completely forgotten the party, *and* Sara; she had filed the actress away in some far-off recess of her mind. Because of guilt? Or did she just hope that by not thinking of the other woman she could make Sara disappear from Philip's life?

"But I told Sara I couldn't go," Lindsay protested, hoping desperately that he would change his mind and stay home, too.

Philip eyed her derisively. "Yes, you did. And as I recall you also told her you had plans for tonight. Don't tell me you're passing up a party to sew those jeans?"

Lindsay remembered her evasion the other afternoon. Still, the last person she wanted to see right now was Sara Warner.

"I really don't want to go, Philip," she told him. "They're your friends. Why don't you go ahead without me?"

Philip stepped into the room, his annoyance more obvious now. "Aren't you being a little ridiculous?" he said. "These are our neighbors, Lindsay. They want to know you. They'll wonder if you don't come."

But one person, at least, will be relieved, thought Lindsay. To Sara, she must be a very unwelcome complication.

She shook her head. "You go, Philip. I'm sure no one will notice if I'm not there."

"Damn it, *I* will," he stated curtly. Then, obviously making an effort to control his temper, his voice softened. "This evening is very important to me, Lindsay. Please come."

Where Philip's insistence had merely strengthened her resolve, the appeal she now saw in his eyes could not be resisted. With a sigh, she put aside her sewing.

"All right. Give me about half an hour to get ready."

The Warner home was nearly filled with party-goers, and when Lindsay saw their formal attire, she was relieved she had finally settled on an elegant gown of the softest russet brown, draped in smooth folds over one creamy shoulder. Despite its deceptively simple cut, she was aware that the dress was very flattering, clinging to her slim figure in all the right places. She had decided to wear her long blond hair loose, letting the soft curls form the perfect frame for her small, oval face. As she expected, most of the guests were strangers, so she was glad when she discovered several members of the *Hedda Gabler* cast in the throng.

Sara was gorgeous in a frothy sky-blue gown, which contrasted strikingly with her fiery auburn hair and fair complexion. Her greeting seemed genuine enough, but Lindsay sensed the underlying strain as the actress's vivid green eyes went first to Philip, then to her.

"I hear you two were stranded on Pakatoa Island last night," she said, and the brightness of her smile could not disguise the deeper query hidden in the words.

She knows, Lindsay thought, suddenly sure the

actress had guessed their secret. But if she had, Sara gave no indication of it as she ushered the two into the living room, performing so many introductions along the way that Lindsay soon lost track.

"Lindsay," she said at last, leading them to a tall, very distinguished gray-haired man in his early sixties, "this is my father, Matthew Warner. Dad, this is Lindsay, Alex's widow."

Had Lindsay imagined it or did the actress put particular emphasis on the word *widow?* Sara was such a fine actress that it was impossible to tell from her face.

"How do you do, Mr. Warner?" she said, shaking the firm hand. "And happy birthday."

The rancher laughed. "I'm not sure birthdays *can* be happy at my age. Still, any excuse to meet with my friends, old *and* new, can't be all bad." He retained possession of Lindsay's hand as he studied her face. "Sara said you were beautiful and she didn't exaggerate. Welcome to God's country, Lindsay."

A becoming hint of color touched Lindsay's cheeks as she returned the farmer's compliment by affectionately squeezing his hand.

"Thank you, Mr. Warner," she said, smiling into the warm, hazel eyes. "I love New Zealand already."

"And it seems you've taken to the land as well. Philip tells me you've joined right in with the work. Not only that, he says you're doing a darn good job."

"I like to be busy," she answered, secretly pleased Philip had thought enough of her efforts to brag about them to their neighbor. "And I enjoy working with my hands." She smiled deprecatingly. "Unfortunately, I still have a tremendous amount to learn about the vineyard."

"Well, get used to it. You'll be learning until your dying day." His hazel eyes twinkled. "But if you ever get tired of crushing grapes, come on over here and I'll give you a few lessons in raising cattle. We can always use a new hand. Especially such a pretty one."

Matthew Warner turned to Philip. "Sara tells me you want to speak to me about something, my boy."

"I do, yes," Philip answered, and Lindsay felt a stab of resentment as he shared a private look with the actress. "It shouldn't take too long. If you don't mind leaving the party for a few minutes?"

The older man slapped a hand onto Philip's back. "You've piqued my curiosity, Philip. We might just as well discuss whatever it is right now. At my age you learn not to put things off." He glanced meaningfully at his daughter. "If only the younger generation would learn that lesson instead of chasing after careers, I might be a grandfather by now." He smiled at Lindsay. "You'll excuse us, won't you, my dear? I'll have these two back out in a minute. Please circulate and enjoy yourself."

But as Lindsay watched the three walk into Matthew Warner's study, she was far from happy. What was so important that Philip and Sara would draw Mr. Warner off in the middle of his birthday party? Then she remembered something Philip had said earlier, when he had first broached the subject of the party in her room. Was this what he'd meant about tonight being of special significance to him? But what could it have to do with Sara, or her dad?

"Well, if it isn't our resident critic," a fuzzy voice said, interrupting her thoughts. Turning, Lindsay found John Maclennan standing by her side, his florid face proclaiming the fact that he'd had several too many drinks. "I'm glad to see you, my dear," he said, his grin decidedly lopsided. "You brought our little production good luck last week. We must invite you to all our opening nights. That is, if you're still here."

"I'll still be here, Mr. Maclennan," she told him. "I plan to stay on in New Zealand."

The director looked surprised. "Well, that's good news." He squeezed her around the waist. "There were those who thought you'd be too bored to stick it out," he went on, the drinks obviously loosening his tongue, "that you were only after whatever money you could get from the place. But I'm glad to hear you're holding on to what belongs to you."

Lindsay felt as if she'd been struck by ice water. Who had said she'd come only for the money? Philip? Sara? The thought that Philip had speculated about her to his friends cut through her heart like a knife.

"Whoever told you that was mistaken," she said stiffly. "I have every intention of staying on and working Kia Ora."

"Good for you!" he boomed. "Spoken like a real trooper." Carefully, he made a study of his glass, then, shaking his head, he executed a little bow. "I see I am in dire need of a refill. I'm afraid I must leave you to your own charming devices."

Lindsay watched as the director's slightly unsteady gait took him in the general direction of the bar; she was still stinging from what he had told her. Surely the man had just had too much to drink. She couldn't believe Philip would say those terrible things, even if he might have suspected her motives at first.

"I was hoping you would come." Lindsay was startled by a hand on her arm and looked up to find Roger Nicolson smiling down at her.

"Roger, I'm glad to see you," she cried, and realized suddenly that the feeling was genuine. The actor was rapidly becoming her refuge in stormy weather, always seeming to be on hand when she needed a friend.

"Where's Philip?" he asked. "Didn't I see him with you a few minutes ago?"

Lindsay nodded toward the study door. "He and Sara are talking to Mr. Warner," she told him.

"It sounds serious. You don't suppose our friends are finally going to make the big announcement, do you?"

Lindsay's heart skipped wildly, but she fought to keep her expression even. "You mean their engagement announcement?"

"Yes, and it's about time, I must say. It can hardly be called a whirlwind courtship. They've known each for centuries. The whole company has been wagering on when they would set the date." He laughed as Lindsay's face blanched, misinterpreting her reaction. "I suppose I sound hopelessly old-fashioned," he went on lightly. "Well, I plead guilty. I still happen to believe in the sanctity of hearth and home." He took her by the elbow and led her through the tightly knotted guests to the next room where the bar was set up. "It looks like I'm also guilty of allowing you to stand there with empty hands. It's obvious you need a drink."

For once Lindsay concurred, and she gratefully accepted a glass from the bartender. Her first gulp was a mistake, though, and she choked as the unaccustomed fluid flowed like fire down her throat. Immediately solicitous, Roger took the drink and patted her back until the spasm passed.

"This is strong medicine," he explained, albeit a bit belatedly as far as Lindsay was concerned. "You're supposed to sip, not gulp it."

"I think I need some air," she gasped, and Roger led her through a maze of guests to double glass doors that opened onto the garden. There, on the spacious veranda, Lindsay finally caught her breath.

"I'm sorry," she apologized, embarrassed to have been so foolish, "but I'm not used to anything that strong."

"That is obvious," said the actor, leading her to a padded love seat overlooking a cluster of graceful ferns. His usual jocularity was suddenly replaced by concern. He cupped her chin in his hand, tilting her face so he could read her eyes in the moonlight. "Now, would you like to tell me what's bothering you, Lindsay? You look as if you've lost your best friend."

Or the man I love, Lindsay thought miserably. She forced a smile as she allowed the actor to kiss her lightly on the lips. Then, as his arm stole around her shoulders, she found she was grateful for the warmth of his presence.

"I'm fine, Roger, really," she said softly, leaning back against the cushioned wicker seat. "I guess I'm just a little tired. Running a vineyard is harder work than it seems."

Roger smiled. "Why do you think I chose acting as a career?"

When Lindsay laughed, the actor brushed his hand over her soft hair. "That's better," he said softly. "You should always laugh. It makes you very beautiful."

For the first time since they'd come out onto the veranda, Lindsay felt uneasy. Was she being unfair to take advantage of Roger's friendship when she had so little to give him in return? As if sensing her thoughts, the actor squeezed her shoulders gently.

"Don't worry, Lindsay," he said gently. "I don't want to rush you. For now, I only want to be your friend."

"I appreciate that, Roger. More than you can imagine." Lindsay shivered, although whether from the cold or from her turbulent emotions she couldn't be sure, and the actor quickly got to his feet.

"We'd better go inside. It's getting chilly out here."

"No, I'd rather not," she said, reluctant to return to the crowd. Or was it Sara and Philip she was afraid to face? For whatever reason, she knew she could not go in just yet.

"Then I'll get your wrap," Roger persisted. "What does it look like?"

Lindsay described the lacy wool shawl she had thrown over her shoulders, and the actor immediately set off to retrieve it. While he was gone, she moved restlessly to the rail of the porch and looked out at the lovely garden beyond. The leafy green and silver ferns melded gracefully with late-blooming orchids and delicate, pink-flowering fuchsia. Farther on in the garden, she could see a grove of beautiful lace-bark trees nearly ready to burst into a snowy show of autumn blossoms.

Then, just in front of the trees, she saw a movement, then a splash of color as two figures were spotlighted in the moonlight. Lindsay could just make out the graceful, upturned line of the woman's face as she lifted it to meet the much taller outline of the man's form. Then they drew together in a long, intimate embrace, and as they kissed Lindsay felt an uneasy stirring inside her. There was something familiar about the couple—the woman's sky-blue dress, the man's darker suit. Then, with a terrible lurch of her heart, she knew. It was Philip and Sara she was watching; they were the lovers stealing a few moments alone in the garden, locked so passionately in each other's arms. Desperately, she wanted to turn away, but it was as if her body were frozen, had lost its ability to move, and she continued to stare in helpless fascination. Finally, long, agonizing minutes later, the two figures parted, but the man's arm remained around the woman's slim waist as they moved off into the trees.

Even then Lindsay could not move; her eyes refused to leave that tranquil refuge in front of the lace-bark trees. But though her body remained rigid, her mind was only too active. What Roger had said was true, then, she thought with surprising calm. Philip had led Sara and her father away to ask for her hand in marriage. Last night and this morning had meant nothing to him. Their lovemaking had been merely a pleasant interlude before the start of his life with Sara. He had used her, manipulated her to suit his own purposes, had gone so far as to joke about her to his friends. Perhaps he had even known there was going to be a storm before taking her to the island last night and had coolly calculated their assignation.

Then she was struck by another thought. Had it all been just a ploy to get her to leave Kia Ora and forfeit her share of Alex's inheritance by making sure she did not remain the full ninety days specified in the will? If that was his plan, it was brilliant. What better way to insure full control of the vineyard than to spurn her for another woman; the woman he had planned to marry all along. What kind of man could do such a thing? Then, with sudden clarity, Lindsay remembered Stephanie's mother. Hadn't he used her, too, taken what he could get until the poor woman was driven to suicide?

The full extent of his callousness spread slowly through her until she felt nothing but fury. She knew that later, when the impact truly hit her, it would be different. Then would come the tears, the bitter heartache. But for now, she drew her wounded pride around her like a protective cloak, desperately hoping it would get her through the next few hours.

When Roger returned with her stole she was ready. Pleading a headache, she asked him to take her home, explaining that she hated to bother Philip under the circumstances. If the actor found her sudden request strange, he said nothing, and Lindsay decided that his easy acceptance, his sensitivity to her feelings, was one of his most attractive features. If only she could love him, she thought bitterly. But her heart seemed forever reserved for a man who held her in total contempt.

"Why did you run off like that?"

Philip's voice was icy cold as it cut through the dim light of the old house. Lindsay, seated stiffly on one of the two straight-backed chairs in the main hallway, had been waiting two hours for his return from the party.

"I want to be the first to congratulate you," she said quietly, ignoring his question.

"For what?" Even in the faint light, Lindsay could see the shadow that crossed his lean face.

"You got what you wanted from Matthew Warner, didn't you?"

"Yes, but how did you know—?"

Bittersweet victory did not assuage the pain in her heart as she went on, her voice still evenly controlled, playing out the most difficult role of her life.

"Roger and I guessed what you were doing," she answered calmly. "It wasn't difficult. I hope everything will work out well for you."

In three long strides, Philip was standing before her chair. "Of course, you realize you're not making any sense," he told her impatiently. "Now it's time for you to answer a question or two. Just what the hell did you mean by going home with Roger Nicolson—without so much as a by-your-leave?"

Lindsay shrugged her slim shoulders. "I didn't think you'd mind. You seemed otherwise occupied." Her brown eyes fixed on his, and even in the dim light her carefully nurtured anger was evident. "I saw you and Sara in the garden," she added simply, as if there were nothing more to be said.

For a moment, his gaze lowered, and she was gratified to see her remark had struck home. "And I suppose you assumed the worst," he said slowly. "Without waiting to hear my side."

"There was no need for an explanation," she countered. "The little scene in the garden spoke for itself."

She stood, no longer able to remain seated under those piercing eyes. "But actually, it's all for the best," she went on, praying she would have the strength to finish what she'd started. "I've been thinking over what happened on the island. It was a mistake, Philip. I think we're both mature enough to admit to that now."

"So to you it was just another casual affair," he told her, his barely controlled fury evident in the pulsating throb in one temple. "A one-night stand. Is that the sort of thing that goes on in Hollywood, Lindsay? Love them and leave them when you get bored?"

"Wait a minute," she broke in, sensing that the scene was getting out of hand.

"No," he rasped, "*you* listen. I want to make sure I've got the scenario straight. Now that you've had your little fling with me you've decided to go running back to your actor friend. You just couldn't resist the lure of the theater, could you, Lindsay? Just like you couldn't resist Alex. Kia Ora must seem pathetically tame in comparison to the life you're used to."

Lindsay's cheeks flamed in the dim light as she longed to scream at the injustice of these words. Who was he to stand in judgment of her after his treachery with Sara not three hours ago? She fought to remain in control, to continue on the course she had set.

"Kia Ora has nothing to do with this," she said, fighting to keep the anger out of her voice. "I'll never leave here no matter what you say or do. Half of this vineyard is mine and, for better or worse, I intend to work it!" Taking a deep breath she tried to calm her racing pulse, tried not to look into those eyes that looked into hers with such contempt. "I simply think it's best if we forget that the episode on the island ever happened."

With a swiftness she could not avoid, he grasped her roughly by the shoulders, holding her so tightly she winced in silent pain.

"Can you forget this?" he demanded, his voice ragged with anger and passion.

Then his lips were on hers, crushing them with a brutal, demanding kiss that took away her breath even as it sent licking flames of desire shooting through her body. With all her strength she fought the rising need to respond, willed her lips to remain still under the bruising, impassioned assault. But she could not stop his tongue from boldly taking possession of her mouth in a blazing journey of conquest. At last her defenses crumbled like so many pieces of clay, and her surrender was complete.

When he finally released her, she stood breathless before him, shaking from this final humiliation. Once again her body had betrayed her, had succumbed to its own despicable longings.

"Do you respond like that to Roger's kisses, Lindsay? Does he put fire in your veins?"

He turned and walked to the stairs, his scathing look shattering the last vestiges of her control. "Or will he simply do, as I did, until something better comes along?"

8

~~~~~~~~~~~~

The next few days passed quickly as life at Kia Ora settled into a kind of pre-harvest frenzy. Philip and Lindsay, although superficially polite, rarely spoke more than a few words to each other. In fact, they almost never came into contact. By the time Lindsay went downstairs for breakfast, he was usually gone, not to return until dinnertime, if then. She assumed his frequent absences in the evening meant he was seeing his fiancée, and it took every ounce of control she possessed to maintain a friendly attitude toward the actress.

For Stephanie's sake, she and Philip pretended all was well between them, but the child's astute looks soon convinced them it was useless. Whenever they were in the same room the tension was so tangible that Lindsay could feel it as a physical barrier keeping them apart. She was sure Stephie could sense it, too, yet she was powerless to hide her torment. Having Philip so near and yet so distant was almost more than she could bear, and she finally came to prefer the nights he went out as being less painful.

Lindsay's routine seldom varied now. Up early, she would spend the morning with Rudy at the winery, fighting to finish the dozens of odd jobs that had to be completed before the actual harvest began. Then, after a quick lunch, it was back to the vineyard until late in the afternoon, when she would stop to give Inia a hand in the kitchen. Since Kiri's departure, Lindsay knew it was difficult for the older woman to take care of the household; but whenever she broached the idea of hired help, the proud housekeeper would not hear of it, insisting she was more than capable of carrying on by herself.

Dinner was usually a quiet affair, with only Stephie's eager chatter to lighten the heavy atmosphere which had settled over them since the night of the party. After supper came the inevitable coffee and chocolate in the den, an interlude that was now, more often than not, spent quietly with Stephie. Then came an hour or so rehearsing the little girl for her part in the play. Lindsay was convinced that this time spent with Stephie, along with the work she was doing in the winery, was all that kept her sane. The child was developing into a talented actress, and Lindsay took pride in the surprisingly professional performance Stephie was soon able to deliver. It was also apparent that she was beginning to love the child as deeply as if she were her own, a fact that, while healthy for Stephie now, might easily lead to later complications.

But basically, without Philip, her days were empty. The warm tingle of expectation she had once experienced whenever she saw him had now developed into a cutting pain in her heart. The scene between Philip and Sara in the garden was etched indelibly in her mind, often playing back in dreams from which she would awake shaken.

Then came the day when there was no more time for brooding, when there simply weren't enough hours in the day for self-pity. The harvest had begun.

If Lindsay thought the pre-harvest bustle trying, she was numbed by the days that followed. True to Rudy's dire predictions, the mechanical harvester's arrival did not coincide with the final ripening stage of the first vines.

"What are we going to do?" Lindsay asked the cellarmaster after she overheard him and Philip discussing the problem one morning.

"We'll go ahead and start without the contraption," the little Irishman told her. "The only problem is that it's too late now to hire the extra hands we need to make up for the machine. Everyone's already committed to the other vineyards."

"Is there danger we'll lose any of the crop?" she asked in alarm.

"That *is* the danger, lass. And one we can hardly afford along with the risk of the new varietals. Somehow we must keep up with the grapes until that harvester gets here or we'll be in deep trouble. And that means usin' every hand we can beg, borrow or steal for as many hours as we can see to work." The little man swept his hand out at the acres of vines surrounding them, patient, as ever, to explain the operation despite his many worries. "You see, for the wine to be right, the grapes have to be picked at just the proper stage of their development. So, machine or not, we have to pick."

Lindsay squinted against the bright morning sun as

she looked out over the hundreds of acres of vines, the branches drooping now from their lush, ripe burden. "Can we do it, Rudy?" she asked seriously. "Will we make it in time?"

The little cellarmaster tilted his elfish head and winked, his grin as infectious as ever. "Of course we'll make it, lass," he told her with his usual optimism. "It'll just be a little harder than we planned."

Lindsay squared her shoulders. "All right," she said tenaciously, "where do I begin?"

Rudy's grin broadened as he looked at her determined face. "So it's pickin' you plan to turn your hand to now, is it? Well, I admire your spirit, lass, but you should know that it's hard, back-breakin' labor you're lettin' yourself in for. You'll think the work we did before was a picnic."

"I have no illusions, Rudy," she answered seriously, "but we're all going to have to pull together if we want to save the crop. You just said so yourself."

The little Irishman chuckled his agreement. "So I did, and as usual you're goin' to hold me to my word, I suppose. Well, don't say that I didn't give you fair warnin'. It's not an easy job you're takin' on." And with that cheerful warning, he handed her a pair of faded, green-cotton gloves. "Here, put these on, lass. You're goin' to need them before the mornin's out."

By late afternoon, Lindsay's back ached painfully, and her arms and shoulders hurt from hauling heavy pans of grapes to a big gondola, or flat trailer, where the fruit was emptied. About three tons later, when the gondola was full, the grapes would be taken into the winery. There, Rudy had explained, they would be pressed, and the *must,* or juice from the crushed grapes, would be pumped into stainless steel tanks where the yeast would be added. After a few days of fermentation, most of the sugar would be transformed into alcohol and they would be ready to start the aging process.

Earlier that morning, Rudy had also pointed out that in order to develop into the best possible wine, the grapes had to be collected with the clusters intact and the skins undamaged and without bruises. Also, the time between picking and the start of actual processing had to be as short as possible, which meant that once they began to fill the gondola, they had to finish the job quickly. Because of the urgency of their task, there was little talk among the pickers; there was simply too much ground to be covered for sociability. Still, there was an implied bond of camaraderie between them, and despite her aches and pains, Lindsay took pleasure in the smiles of encouragement extended toward her as she labored.

That night she slept more soundly than she had in weeks, a heavy, dreamless slumber from which she rose before dawn the next morning. Although her weary muscles protested the unaccustomed labor, she was ready to commence the new day, eager to meet the challenge that threatened the vineyard's future. Gratefully accepting the bag lunch Inia prepared for her, she set off for the fields before the sun had barely peeked over the horizon.

As she worked, Lindsay marveled at her more seasoned fellow pickers, the best of whom, she knew, were averaging up to 2,000 pounds of grapes a day. She noticed that they sprinted through the long rows of vines during the early morning hours, picking and hauling as quickly as possible, then eased off during the heat of the day, collecting at a more comfortable, though still lively, pace. Her own steady plodding seemed pathetically slow by comparison. Still, she consoled herself as she bent nearly double beneath the next vine, every pair of hands helped.

"Not bad. You're developing into a fairly passable picker."

Lindsay was so startled to hear the low, painfully familiar voice that she suddenly straightened, momentarily forgetting the thick, tough stems above her head.

"Ouch," she cried, as a thorny growth scratched down the side of her neck, drawing a thin trickle of blood.

Instantly, Philip was by her side. "Here," he said, "let me have a look at that."

His touch fired her skin like an electric current, and instinctively she drew back. Looking as if she'd slapped him in the face, Philip frowned.

"I'm not being personal," he told her shortly. "If that cut isn't taken care of it could become infected. And then we'd be out a worker."

"And of course we couldn't have that," she replied, matching his tone. "Still, I can take care of it myself."

But it was too late; he had already turned back toward the pickup, returning in a moment with the first-aid kit.

"I'm not going to risk losing a good hand just because you feel like being stubborn," he told her, sitting her down firmly on an overturned pail.

Very gently, he bathed the scratch with antiseptic, then rocked back on his heels as he studied the wound.

"You're lucky, it's not very deep. You know, you should be more careful where you poke your head while you're picking."

"And you shouldn't startle people like that," she countered. Deliberately, Lindsay turned back to her work, her agitation lending speed to her fingers. She could feel Philip watching her as she picked, but purposely she kept her eyes diverted, concentrating on the heavy clusters of grapes.

"You know you really *are* getting good at that," he said at last, and she was pleased to detect a note of surprise in his voice. "Are you sure you've never done this before?"

Lindsay continued working as she answered. "No, but I've picked enough corn to spread from here to Auckland. It's not all that different."

He was silent for so long that she thought he had gone back to the truck, and she felt an irrational pang of disappointment. Then she heard a rustle of leaves beside her and realized he was picking, too, depositing the clusters expertly in a fresh pail every bit as quickly as the veteran pickers.

"You're not bad yourself," she said, and felt unaccountably light-headed when he grinned back at her over a vine.

"You could stretch out the grapes I've picked over the years next to your corn," he said, his hands moving agilely over the clusters. "My uncle taught me to pick grapes about the same time I learned to walk."

It was the first time he had mentioned his childhood, and Lindsay listened with interest as he told her how he had come to live at Kia Ora after the death of his parents when he was three. Then her thoughts went to Alex, the inimical cousin whose very name fired Philip's temper. Had Alex been taught by his father to pick from early childhood, too? Somehow, she could not imagine the free-living Alex out here in the fields picking grapes from sunrise to sunset, feeling the dust in his throat and the sun in his face. Poor Alex, she thought dolefully. His life at Kia Ora must have been a tragic mismatch from the beginning.

As they picked, Lindsay felt more lighthearted than

she had in days. Despite their differences, it seemed right having Philip by her side, working together toward a common goal. How different it might be, she thought ruefully, if only he returned her love, if his heart was not committed to the beautiful Sara Warner. For as she watched the handsome dark head bend toward the grapes, and the long, strong fingers move surely at their task, she realized how very much she still loved Philip, would always love him no matter what came between them. But what could she do? How could she fight all those years he had shared with the actress, those years of his life she could never be a part of? How could she compete?

No matter how many times Lindsay asked herself these questions she found no answers in the exhausting days that followed. Suddenly the world seemed composed of endless rows of vines, limitless clusters of grapes and backbreaking hours of labor, relieved only by a few druglike hours of blessed sleep every night before the same agonizing cycle began again before dawn the next morning. Yet despite all their efforts, the battle was getting away from them.

"We're just not keepin' up," Rudy told her the next week. "Nature's holdin' all the trump cards, lass, and the vines are ripenin' faster than we can pick." He shook his wiry head. "I only hope that machine gets here soon."

As did everyone. With indomitable stubbornness, they voluntarily doubled work schedules that were already too long, extending their hours in the fields to make use of every second of light, picking until Lindsay thought she surely would drop. She could not remember ever being so tired, not even during her days on the farm, yet her whole being seemed obsessed with the will to win, to be victorious in this breakneck race against time. Everyone on the vineyard pitched in. Stephie insisted on being allowed to miss school for a few days to help, and Lindsay was surprised to find the child a welcome addition to their work force. She even spied Inia's salt and pepper head bobbing up and down in the field and was struck by the intense love they all shared for Kia Ora.

As the weary hours melded into exhausting days, Lindsay frequently looked up from her labors to find Philip working by her side, his quiet determination lending strength to them all. She knew, as they all did, that he was driving himself harder than anyone, sleeping fewer hours and carrying the lion's share of the worry. But other than a subtle darkness beneath his eyes and a tightening of the muscles around his mouth, he gave no sign of the strain he was under. And Lindsay knew with a certainty beyond hope that she was falling more helplessly in love with him every day.

Then, suddenly, it was over and, miraculously, they had won. Nature might have held the cards, but their love and dedication had been enough to restack the deck. They had stayed ahead of the game. Then, anticlimactically, the mechanical harvester arrived, a huge, arrogant steel monster to replace bruised and battered flesh. And as Lindsay watched the blind fingers of the machine shake the vines clean, she felt a loss, a relinquishing of something pure and simple to the relentless wheels of progress.

"How can you trust that machine to pick the grapes when we had to be so careful not to break the skins?" she asked Rudy one afternoon as they watched the machine's oscillating batons shake the berries onto conveyor belts and then into a gondola running along an adjoining row.

"We can't trust it with most of the grapes," the little Irishman answered, "since the skins often do get broken when the machine shakes them off. But it works very well with the Cabernet Sauvignon and Chardonnay berries because their skins are tougher than average. And since these grapes account for most of the new vines Mr. Philip put in, a mechanical harvester seemed a worthwhile investment." The cellarmaster winked at her cheerfully. "But don't worry, lass. We'll continue to pick nearly seventy percent of the crop by hand. You've still got your job."

And, true to his word, the picking continued. Even though the harvester removed much of the pressure, the hand picking still went on from early morning until late in the afternoon. Lindsay noticed, though, that the workers soon settled back into a more comfortable, easily sustained pace. Within a very short period of time, life in the Kia Ora fields was much as it had been before the crisis.

But, for Lindsay, it was not the same. Something irretrievable had been lost. Gone were Philip's unexpected and comforting appearances when he would work for hours by her side, allowing her to share, if only for a brief time, his life and his dreams. And gone, too, was the temporary suspension of hostilities between them.

Although nothing formal had been said, Philip's attitude the past two weeks, during their desperate battle against time and nature, had softened. When he'd looked at her over the vines, there had been approval in those dark eyes, real acceptance of her labors, a camaraderie she came to treasure. Their time together in the fields, working side by side to save the vintage, had become somehow more intimate to her than the hours they'd spent on Pakatoa Island, and each precious moment among the vines was now carefully stored away to become the stuff of her dreams. For as soon as the harvest was assured it was as if a light had gone out in his eyes, and once again she felt an almost palpable strain in their relationship. Now when he looked at her it was as if she were once again the interloper, and something inside Lindsay mourned for what had been and was now forever lost.

Then, just before the end of the harvest, and several weeks after its hectic beginning, the harvester turned all their lives around with frightening abruptness.

The day began innocuously enough, the morning very cool now that summer was past, the afternoon fraught with biting winds and occasional rains, making the final autumn picking more difficult. Lindsay was pleased to see that the novelty of the giant machine had finally worn off, and the parade of workers stealing glimpses of the harvester had ended, leaving only those actually involved in the operation. It was late, and dusk was beginning to fall as tired, chilled workers prepared to wind up the day's picking. Lindsay was gathering the few odd clusters of Cabernet Sauvignon grapes that had withstood the relentless steel fingers of the machine as she watched Rudy supervise tractor-gondola teams working in relays to keep pace with the harvester. As she looked on, she couldn't help marveling at how quickly and smoothly the Irishman had a second gondola moved into place as soon as the first one was filled, its contents already being rushed to the winery. With a sigh, Lindsay realized that the cellarmaster, like the rest of them, was adapting to the new, even as he pined for the old.

She saw Michael Taira atop the cab of the harvester, his able hands guiding the machine's progress down the long rows. The speed of the machine, a plodding but steady one-half mile per hour, reminded Lindsay of a very slow, giant tractor as it lumbered through the vines, and she thought of the machines that plowed the fields back home. There was something comfort-

ing, if a little frightening, about the long steel append-
ages as they monotonously stretched out along the
bordering trellis, shaking free the grapes. Then, even
as she stood mesmerized by the ponderous machine,
it stopped, grinding the rest of the operation to a halt
with it.

"What's the matter?" she heard Rudy ask the
young Maori from his position in an adjacent row.

"I don't know," Michael replied, moving several
controls. "The engine's still running. It must be stuck
on something."

Effortlessly, the young man swung himself down
from the cab and walked slowly around the machine.
Then, apparently finding nothing wrong, he stepped
under the high belly of the harvester, his dark eyes
scanning every inch of steel as he walked.

"Can you find what's wrong, lad?" the cellarmaster
called out again.

Without answering, the Maori squatted to better
look beneath one of the wheels. "I think I found it," he
yelled back to Rudy. "The clutch seems to be
jammed." Bent nearly double, Michael banged the
clutch with his fist. Then, having no success, he
reached out to kick the clutch plate with his foot.

"Stop," called out a familiar voice, and Lindsay
whirled around to see Philip jump out of the pickup,
which he'd pulled to a stop just behind the harvester.
"Don't try to move anything until you've set the
brake!" he yelled, running over to Michael.

But it was too late. Already the huge machine had
begun to roll, trapping the Maori's foot beneath the
heavy wheels. With a scream of pain, the young man
fell to his knees, pulling frantically at his imprisoned
leg. Then, before anyone could move, there were
suddenly two bodies beneath the harvester, and Lindsay watched in frozen terror as Philip struggled against

the unyielding monster. With a superhuman heave, he finally snatched Michael from beneath the harvester and flung him over to one side, safe from the ongoing roll of the vehicle. But the effort cost Philip his precarious balance, and the workers watched in horror as his right sleeve was drawn inexorably into the mechanism of the machine.

"For God's sake, stop the harvester!" Lindsay cried, fear lending speed to her legs as she flew toward the machine. With a strength she hardly knew she possessed, she scrambled up the side of the cab, then grasped for the lever Rudy had explained earlier was the emergency brake. With all her might she pulled it toward her, praying that it would not be too late, that Philip wasn't already crushed.

And then it was over. The harvester was finally still, its two victims, safe now, laid carefully in the back of the pickup, their bodies gently covered with a soiled blanket someone had found in the field. Rudy himself drove, as if he trusted no one else, and beside him, one of the vineyard foremen rode in stricken silence. But in the bed of the truck only Lindsay kept the lonely vigil as they sped toward the hospital, her face nearly as colorless as those of the two men who lay so ominously still beneath the tattered blanket.

"But it's been nearly an hour," she told the nurse. "Surely there's some word by now."

The nurse, a kindly woman in her midforties, looked up from her work and smiled. "I can understand your anxiety, Mrs. Macek," she said gently. "But both Mr. Taira and your husband are still undergoing emergency treatment. I'll let you know the moment we hear anything definite."

Lindsay smiled weakly, not having the strength to correct the woman's error. Of course she would be mistaken for Philip's wife, she thought desolately. They shared the same name; it was a natural enough mistake. Then, miserably, Lindsay wished with all her heart that the nurse's words could be true.

Despite the woman's promise, they waited without word for another hour. During that time, Rudy talked nonstop, as if by keeping them occupied he could make sure there'd be no time to speculate on what was happening in the emergency room. But, however noble the little Irishman's intentions, Lindsay found the incessant chatter nerve-wracking and was relieved when the two men finally decided to go down to the cafeteria for a quick cup of coffee. Refusing their offer to join them, she took to pacing the modern, sterile-looking room, trying to keep her worst fears at bay. What could be taking so long? Why didn't they send out word, *any* word? No, she amended quickly, she'd rather wait and hear good news. Philip had to be all right. The thought of losing him was more than she could bear.

Then, with a start, she realized that losing Philip was exactly what she'd been prepared to do. Since the party at the Warners' she'd been resigned to giving Philip up forever to the lovely actress. Not until this afternoon, when there'd been a very real threat to his life, had she realized how desperately she wanted and needed him. Lindsay stopped pacing and leaned her forehead against the cool glass of the waiting-room window, her tears blurring the steady stream of evening traffic still bustling by on the busy streets below. If only he pulled through, she vowed, she would do everything in her power to make him love her as totally as she loved him.

"Hey, why the tears?" a voice said softly. "Is this some kind of a wake?"

Lindsay gasped to see Philip standing just beside

her, his right arm drawn up into a sling, his dark eyes as lightly mocking as ever.

"Philip—thank God you're all right!" Without thinking, she stood on tiptoe and threw her arms around his neck, deluging his face with kisses. It wasn't until he gave an involuntary moan that she remembered his injuries. "Oh, your arm, I'm sorry," she cried, pulling back in alarm. "I didn't mean to hurt you." She took him gently by the other hand and led him to a couch. "Here, let's sit down. Tell me how bad it is."

"There was no need to stop just now," he grinned. "I was rather enjoying the attention. It makes all that folderol in there almost worthwhile." He pointed playfully at a spot on his right cheek. "You can resume your commiseration right here."

Cheered by his high spirits, Lindsay planted a generous kiss on the indicated spot while Philip's good left arm stole around her waist.

"You still haven't told me how seriously injured your arm is," she chided, sternly refusing to be drawn any deeper into his embrace. "And why were you in there so long?"

"At the risk of losing all this tender loving care, there doesn't seem to be much wrong with me other than a few minor scratches and bruises." He gazed ruefully at his torn clothes. "And a ruined shirt, of course." Then, as Lindsay looked pointedly at the sling, he smiled. "Well, perhaps a few pulled muscles, too. But the X rays showed no broken bones, so I'll be back in the fields in no time. And to answer your second question, they wouldn't let me out of their fiendish clutches until they were sure I was suffering no more than a mild concussion from banging my head on the harvester. I'm assured that as soon as my headache's gone I'll be good as new." He grinned down at her. "Now, are you satisfied?"

"Yes, thank God," she breathed. "I was so worried."

His eyes scanned hers questioningly. "That's obvious. *And* surprising. I had no idea you cared one whit what happened to me. In fact, you made your feelings on the subject very clear the night of Sara's party. Why the sudden change?"

Lindsay's heart was so full she was afraid her emotions would spill over, and the last thing Philip needed right now was hysterics.

"Not here," she said, embarrassed. "We can talk about it at home." Then her face grew serious again as she suddenly remembered the young Maori. "What about Michael? How is he?"

"He's awake now, although I'm afraid his concussion is a good deal worse than mine. And he's got a pretty badly broken leg where it was twisted by the machine. He'll have to spend several weeks in traction. But the doctor assures me his young bones will mend quickly and he doesn't expect any complications. As a matter of fact, we can go in to see him in a few minutes."

Rudy and his foreman returned from their coffee just in time to join them as they walked to Michael's room. The obvious relief in the Irishman's eyes was touching when he saw his boss standing in the waiting room. Still, the cellarmaster kept his voice light and matter-of-fact as he slapped an arm around Philip's good shoulder.

"I can see that it takes more than a piece of machinery to put you out of commission," he told him jauntily as they started down the hall. "Still, you can thank this young lady and her quick reflexes for stoppin' that contraption before it took off with you down the field. It all happened so fast the rest of us seemed to have our feet glued to the ground."

Philip looked sharply at Lindsay, and she blushed under his penetrating gaze.

"I used to drive the tractors at home," she explained, embarrassed by the sudden attention. "And fortunately Rudy gave me a ride in the harvester shortly after it arrived, so I was familiar with the controls."

"Still," Rudy continued with evident pride, "you were the one who got there first." He shook his head. "Never have I seen a body move so fast. I wouldn't have thought it possible."

"Nor would I," Philip agreed slowly, his extraordinary eyes studying her closely. "Rudy, this young woman is full of surprises, wouldn't you say?"

"Aye, sir," the little Irishman said with alacrity. "She is, and that's a fact."

It was well after eleven when they arrived back at Kia Ora, but Inia and Stephanie were both waiting patiently for them in the kitchen, a pot of coffee still hot on the stove.

"I know you said Mr. Philip and Michael were all right when you called from the hospital," the housekeeper said as she settled them at the table. "But Stephie and I had to see for ourselves that it was true."

"Oh, Papa," the child cried, crawling carefully into his lap, "we were so worried." She examined his arm, which hung stiffly in the sling. "Are you sure it's not broken?" she asked doubtfully.

Philip kissed the little girl gently on her cheek, then slipped his left arm around her warm flannel pajamas.

"It's just bruised, Peanut," he told her cheerfully, "and in a few days I'll be good as new." He gave her a

146

little squeeze, then set her on her feet. "And now that you know you're still stuck with your old dad, I think it's high time you were in bed. How can you be bright eyed for school tomorrow without any sleep?"

"Oh, Papa, tomorrow's Saturday," the child chided. Then, at her father's grin, she laughed. "You're just teasing, aren't you? You know tomorrow's the play." Then she grew serious. "But you're right, Papa. If I want to give my best performance I'd better get to bed. After all, it's opening night." She ran around the table and kissed Lindsay and then Inia good night before giving her father one final hug. "But you'd better turn in too, Papa. Inia says you should get lots of rest after all you've been through."

Philip looked at his daughter, but Lindsay knew his next words were meant for her. "I'm not sure that sleep is what I need most, Peanut," he smiled. "But don't worry, I intend to find just the right therapy."

"Weren't you a little obvious down there?" Lindsay asked a short while later as she stood in Philip's bedroom and helped him off with his torn shirt.

It was the first time she had been in his room, but she was not surprised to find it very masculine: massive oak furniture, including a large, somewhat disarranged bookcase and warm, coffee-brown carpeting, accented by an attractive brown and rust-colored spread on the king-size bed. On the walls she was amazed to find several really good gold etchings, hung with narrow dark wood frames at tasteful intervals. In the adjoining bath, she could just see Philip's toilet articles laid out on the dark beige tile counter, and the scent of his aftershave was sensuously pungent in the air. Overall, the room had a neat but comfortably lived-in feeling, a very accurate reflection of the man who inhabited it, Lindsay decided.

She tried to hide her discomfiture at being in this very masculine stronghold by keeping her presence there on a strictly impersonal basis. Philip needed help and she was happy to give it—it need not go beyond that. But the overpowering effect of his nearness, coupled with her profound relief that he was safe, acted like a drug on her senses, and she was feeling dangerously light-headed.

"Why shouldn't I be obvious?" he was saying as she worked. "Anyone can see I need help during my incapacitation." He brushed his lips through her hair as she bent her head to rip off the last remnants of the tattered shirt. "Besides, you owe me complete servitude."

Lindsay looked up in surprise. "And how did you reach that remarkable conclusion?"

"You saved my life, of course. It's an old Maori custom that when someone saves another's life the knight, or in this case, *lady* errant, must forever after take responsibility for that person's well-being."

"I don't believe that for one minute," Lindsay scoffed, continuing with her ministrations and refusing the temptation to look up into those sultry blue eyes. "You're bending tradition to suit your own desires."

Lindsay caught her breath as Philip's remaining good arm drew her tightly into his bare chest.

"That's exactly what I'm doing," he breathed, burying his head in her soft hair. "And I desire you very much." Without releasing his hold, he brushed his lips along her cheek, then beneath her hair to the nape of the neck.

Of their own accord, her arms stole around him, rejoicing in the lean, sinewy power she felt rippling beneath her exploring fingers, treasuring the warm, virile body that had been so nearly snatched from her mere hours ago. Wantonly she let her hands roam, let them wander over his shoulders, his back, then, willfully, allowed them to come to rest on the waist of his jeans. Philip moaned huskily in her ear as her slim body pressed against his, her passion barely controlled now as she clearly felt his heightened desire.

"Don't you think it's time we started my therapy?" he whispered. Without waiting for her assent, he led her to the oversized bed, which dominated one wall of the large room.

Smoothly, considering his injured arm, he laid her back against the covers, easing himself down beside her. Then, with a need too long suppressed, his lips found hers and she savored the sensuous glide of his tongue as it moved boldly, uninhibitedly to possess her mouth until she responded with an abandoned urgency of her own.

As their bodies came together she felt the erratic beat of their hearts as they blended into an electrifying tempo of desire. Every part of her clamored for his touch, his kisses, and she arched closer in a desperate need to be united with him, to salve the longing which threatened to consume her. Gone were the doubts and the resolutions. As long as they could be together like this it was possible to forget both the past and the future. Only the present had any substance, any meaning. With a sigh of surrender, Lindsay felt the lovely, spiraling descent into that other plane of time and existence, when all that mattered was her love, her longing, their mutual fulfillment in each other's arms.

"I need you," he breathed, and Lindsay pressed forward to meet that need with a corresponding hunger of her own.

With impatient fingers, she unfastened his belt buckle, then smoothed his pants down until he lay next to her naked, his very male body a perfect symmetry of lean, hard muscles beneath the tanned flesh. Then, slowly, with her help, he undressed her, his mouth and tongue following his one good hand as it carefully stripped away each impediment. One full breast, then the other, became the captive of his eager teeth, and they teased and massaged the pink nipples into rigid peaks of desire. Then his marauding lips explored further, moving with moist licks of fire across the warm, sensitive regions of her body, until her entire being was flamed by an inferno of longing.

Even as her mind screamed caution, her body was powerless to withstand the onslaught of his passion. Eagerly, desperately, it responded to his touch, his kiss, until, at the very precipice of desire, they were joined, became one, in an act as old as time.

"Love me, Philip," she groaned, her whole being feverish for the satisfaction only he could bring. "Love me, please!"

Then, with unerring precision, their bodies melded together in the powerful, rhythmic thrust of his hips, until, finally, they were lost in a buffeting, raging sea of ecstasy, culminating in boundless waves of fulfillment.

Long after she heard the deep, even flow of Philip's breathing, Lindsay lay awake in the darkness, savoring the splendor of the moment they had just shared. With a longing born of desperation, she wished it could always be like this, his arms warm and safe about her. Gently, she reached out and smoothed the covers over his injured arm. Then, as her hand touched his bare skin, she knew suddenly that she loved him with an intensity that went beyond reason, wanted him with a desire she could never feel for another man.

The last doubts were removed. With a firm sense of

purpose, Lindsay knew she did not want to lose Philip; despite the lovely Sara Warner, she must not give him up without a fight. And as she closed her eyes at last, it was with the sure knowledge that she would do everything in her power to keep Philip Macek *and* Kia Ora.

9

When, almost as a body, the audience in the small auditorium rose for a standing ovation, Lindsay knew she was not alone in her enthusiasm for the production. It really had been well done; the play itself, an original written by the school drama coach, was humorous yet with its share of pathos, the acting far above average for a group of nine- and ten-year-olds. Of course, as far as Lindsay was concerned, the incontestable star of the show had been Stephanie, and she was delighted to see that the audience agreed, according the child rousing applause when she stood alone for the final bow. Blushing furiously beneath her stage makeup, Stephanie graciously acknowledged her fans with several more bows than had been required of anyone else in the cast. And as the child bent her dark head for the fourth time, Lindsay met Philip and Inia's eyes and knew they all shared Stephie's triumph.

If the opening-night cast party, immediately following the production, lacked some of the glamour and sophistication of the *Hedda Gabler* affair, it had more than its share of enthusiasm and noise. Exuberant fourth- and fifth-graders served punch and sweets to their families and friends as they basked in their brief, but well-deserved, moment of glory. The play would be performed one more night and then all the work and worry, as well as all the fun, would be over. But one thing would not end with the final performance. The shy, restrained child Lindsay had met only weeks ago was now a charming, outgoing young lady, and Lindsay was intensely proud of her protégée.

But perhaps the best news of the evening came after they arrived back at Kia Ora. There, waiting rather apprehensively in the kitchen, was Kiri, two well-worn suitcases standing, still unpacked, by the door. From the woebegone expression on the girl's pretty face, Lindsay gathered that her venture into the world of modeling had been somewhat less than successful.

"I read in the papers that Michael had been hurt," she said, explaining her sudden reappearance. "I've already been to the hospital and he told me how worried you've all been about me."

"Where have you been?" Inia asked, the relief on her broad face belying the sharpness of her tone.

"Not very far, Mama," the girl answered in a small voice. "I only got as far as Auckland. When I left I meant to get a job and save enough to go to Australia." She looked crestfallen. "But I just couldn't seem to get ahead. Keeping the apartment and eating took everything I made."

Inia's deep brown eyes reflected her pain. "But why did you leave like that?" she asked, more gently this time.

"I guess I just wanted to make something of my-self," the girl said softly. "Seeing all those fashion models in the magazines made it look so easy." Her young face looked so vulnerable that Lindsay's heart ached for her anguish. "But the only job I could find was as a waitress. When I tried the modeling agencies they said I needed a portfolio—and some experience. But I couldn't get one without the other. I just kept going round in circles." There were tears in her large brown eyes as she looked up at her mother. "I'm really sorry about worrying you, Mama. I wanted to make you so proud of me."

Inia's face softened, and she swept a strong arm around her daughter's shoulders. "I am proud of you, girl," she said. "It's me I'm ashamed of—for not understanding how much all this meant to you. I tried to force my way of life onto you and that was wrong. I realized that after you were gone." She held her daughter at arm's length, and looked intently into her face. "If you still want to try modeling, honey, I'll do everything I can to help you get started."

Kiri laughed through her tears and hugged her mother tightly. "I guess I've learned something, too, Mama. I missed you so much. I even missed your scolding. And Michael—I never dreamed how lonely I would be without him. When I heard he'd been hurt, well, I just couldn't stay away any longer." Kiri lifted her small chin, and Lindsay could see the mother's proud determination reflected in her daughter's young face. "I still want to make it on my own, Mama. But not like that. Next time I want to plan ahead and do it right. And I want your blessing."

Lindsay found a catch in her throat that prevented words, but Stephanie had no such impediment.

"Hurray!" the child cried, and ran to throw her arms around the Maori girl. "I'm so glad you're back,

154

Kiri. Please don't go away again." They all laughed at the child's buoyant spirits. "Now that you're back you can see the play tomorrow night. It's a big success. Just wait until you see the costumes!"

"We'll all go, Peanut," Philip said, swooping the little girl up into his strong arms. "It isn't every day a star is born in the Macek family."

But Philip was not to see the closing performance of Stephanie's play after all. He and Lindsay had hardly settled the excited child in bed when Inia called them back downstairs. In the kitchen, they found the housekeeper and an agitated Rudy Corrigan, his weary face reflecting the long hours he was putting in to wrap up the harvest.

"It's the filler," he told them without preamble. "Workin' right as rain for weeks and now all of a sudden it's gone temperamental on us. I thought you'd better have a look."

Without a word, Philip hurried out the back door with a tight-lipped Rudy close behind. Throwing a sweater over her shoulders, Lindsay quickly followed the men's long strides to the winery and into the bottling room. There, a night shift was processing the newly fermented wine into bottles on a huge machine called the German Seitz filler. The atmosphere in the normally noisy room was ominously quiet, and as she looked at the dozens of bottles, standing like so many silent, stiff soldiers in their ranks, she realized with a sinking heart that Rudy had not exaggerated the problem.

"What's the matter?" she asked the little cellarmaster as Philip moved quickly to inspect the conveyor.

"I wish I knew, lass," he sighed, and Lindsay was dismayed by the new lines of worry etched deeply around his light blue eyes. "One minute it was workin' smooth as you could want and the next, kerflooie," he snapped his fingers, "nothin'."

"But isn't this one of the new machines?"

"It is—just put in this year. That's the trouble with mechanization, lass," he said dispiritedly. "It generally means there's that much more to go wrong."

"I know it's part of the bottling line, but what exactly does this section do?" she asked, awed by the impressive length of steel gadgetry.

"It's step one of the new bottlin' procedure," he answered patiently, as he watched Philip and the line foreman go over every inch of the machine. "The wine travels under pressure from the bottlin' tanks to the filler here. But since the bottles have to be absolutely clean and oxygen-free, they're filled with nitrogen first. Then the wine flows into the bottle displacin' the nitrogen before it goes on to have the cork put in. It sounds complicated but it's a lot faster than the old ways. That is, when it's workin'," he added wryly. "When everythin's goin' right it fills about forty bottles a minute."

Lindsay looked at the stationary bottles, a discouraging sight when they'd worked so hard to rush the grapes in from the field. "What happens when it bogs down like this?"

"The same thing that happened when the harvester was late, lass," the cellarmaster told her. "We do the job with our own two God-given hands."

Which is what they did, or at least tried to do. Philip and Rudy worked all night on the ailing filler, finally giving up the effort shortly before dawn.

"I think we finally located the difficulty," a very tired Philip told her at breakfast. "But I'll have to go to the source for the replacement part. These machines are so new there's just no place closer than the manufacturer that stocks what we need. Besides, I'll have to spend some time in Germany learning how the darn thing works so we can do the repairs when I get back." At her surprised look, he went on, "If that filler isn't fixed in the next few days all our hard work in the fields will literally go down the drain. With any kind of luck I'll be back in two days."

But it was nearly four days before Philip returned with the necessary parts. Stephanie's play had closed three days earlier in a blaze of glory, and two nights after that *Hedda Gabler* drew to an end. But aside from a couple of hours stolen at the school for the little girl's concluding performance, Lindsay spent most of her time at the winery, lending a hand to the tedious task of manual bottling. When she wasn't working there, she was busy preparing for the harvest celebration, which was now only a few days off. There, fortunately, she had Inia and Kiri's years of experience to help guide her through the multitude of last-minute arrangements.

And each day the tension grew more tangible. The main topic of conversation around the winery now, aside from the broken filler machine, was the fate of the varietals. It was common knowledge throughout the vineyard that the future of Kia Ora was bound inextricably to the success or failure of the new wines. As the day of the celebration drew closer, anticipation built to an almost fever pitch as each worker pondered the probability of his future employment. And Lindsay worried with the rest. She prayed desperately that the varietals would be everything Philip hoped for, that they would prove to be New Zealand's first really great wine.

For the workers weren't the only ones whose lives would be touched by the experiment, she realized. As she lay alone those nights Philip was away and longed for the warmth of his arms, missed him with an ache that was nearly unendurable, she knew her future, too, was inescapably bound to the new varietals, and to their innovative creator. All their efforts, their sacrifice, had to be enough. They couldn't fail now. The new wine must be a success.

"Sara says we're going to celebrate both our plays at the harvest party Saturday," Stephie told her the morning of the day Philip was expected to return. "Won't that be wonderful?"

Mutely, Lindsay nodded, chilled more by the mention of the actress's name than by all the difficulties confronting them on the vineyard. For several days she had managed not to think about Sara, had been so busy she'd been able to push their beautiful neighbor out of her mind. Had the vintner been able to do the same, she wondered? How did he feel about the glamorous actress in view of his present relationship with her? Was it possible he and Sara might still announce their engagement at the end of the week?

Of course there were no answers to these questions. Philip was still gone and pride prevented her from any direct confrontation with the actress. She could only go on from day to day, doing what had to be done, fighting once again to save the vintage, and, most important, wait for Philip's return and the encounter that was now inevitable. And through it all she continued with plans for the harvest celebration, an occasion that now loomed before her as a multi-headed threat to her happiness.

And then he was back, but frustratingly, there was no time to broach the subject uppermost in her mind. For nearly two days the men grappled with the filler machine, replacing defective parts with new ones, lubricating, cleaning, cursing, until, finally, it was once again operating with its former noisy efficiency. Still, there was no opportunity to be alone with Philip. Out-of-town guests for the next day's celebration had already begun to arrive: several distributors from as far away as Australia were to be present for the grand unveiling of the new varietals, as well as local business acquaintances from Wellington and South Island's larger towns of Christchurch and Dunedin. A number of people were expected from Auckland tomorrow, as well as personal friends and neighbors from the entire Henderson Valley community. Harvest's end at Kia Ora promised to be a day of great celebration. Lindsay could only wonder if it would prove to be a day of intense heartbreak as well.

The day of the party dawned as bright and clear as any of them dared hope. After breakfast, Lindsay set out to complete a myriad of last-minute preparations. Stephie, nearly bursting with anticipation, skipped here and there, offering her services to anyone patient enough to accept them. Mainly, she attached herself to Lindsay, following her about the house and yard like a faithful, playful puppy. But the child's enthusiasm was contagious, and as the morning wore on, Lindsay found that despite her trepidation she, too, was becoming excited about this afternoon's gathering.

By noon everything was ready: the garden area was decorated with bright crepe streamers and balloons, the many tables arranged throughout the garden covered with spotless linen and gaily set for the impending feast. Along the wide veranda, Lindsay displayed the many elaborate and beautiful Maori wood carvings and crafts contributed by their friends and neighbors for the occasion. A wooden platform along the far side of the garden had been erected to house a five-piece Maori ensemble, which was already busy tuning its instruments and setting up several native-looking drums. And from the enthusiastic sounds already emanating from that direction, Lindsay guessed they would be a very lively group.

Along the side of the bandstand, a large table had been set aside for sampling the vintage, most of the cases of wine resting in the shade of the porch, while some of the sweeter whites cooled in the refrigerator. Over all, delicious aromas issued from both the kitchen and a wide pit that had been dug just off the garden. It was in this pit that most of their meat was steam-cooking beneath the earth, luau style.

"You've done a fantastic job," Philip told her, as he stopped in the kitchen on his way upstairs to change. Even now, just minutes before the party was to begin, he was still wearing work clothes, his sprained right arm well enough now to be out of a sling. Business first, Lindsay thought resignedly. We may be celebrating the bountiful harvest this afternoon, but Philip and the men are still out there making it happen.

He cupped her face in one hand and combed long, strong fingers through her fine blond hair with the other. Bending his head, he brushed her lips with a kiss, then pressed against them more earnestly as he pulled her slim body into his. Responding with all the loneliness of the past few days, Lindsay moved her mouth eagerly against his, feeling deliriously at home in his arms, safe at last from the doubts that had assailed her during his absence.

"I missed you, partner," he told her, releasing her lips but continuing to hold her around the waist. "It was good knowing you were here to hold things together while I was gone."

With another quick kiss, this time on the cheek, he turned and hurried upstairs, leaving Lindsay behind to wonder at his words. Had he missed her only in a professional sense? Was she important simply because she helped hold things together when he was gone? What *did* she mean to him? she asked herself for the hundredth time.

There was little time for more of these somber thoughts, as the next hour was filled with new arrivals and seemingly endless introductions. Everyone appeared to know her, or to have at least heard of her, while she labored under the distinct disadvantage of being familiar with only a few of their visitors. She was delighted to see Richard Hansen, the enologist from Auckland, and was even more pleased when he handed her a large bouquet of bright yellow chrysanthemums.

"To my favorite corn farmer," he said jauntily. He looked around at the crowd milling about the festive garden. "I heard you've had your share of problems, but everthing seems to be under control now."

"Finally," Lindsay laughed. "But I don't think I've ever worked so hard in my life. Not even on the farm."

"Glad to see you're developing a healthy appreciation of the happy life of the vintner." He grinned. "Now, lead me to the vintage and I'll pronounce my verdict."

Lindsay left Richard happily sampling at the table where all but the varietals were laid out for inspection. She was just returning to the kitchen when she felt a hand slip around her slim waist.

"You look ravishingly beautiful as usual," Roger Nicolson said, his eyes roaming appreciatively over the trim lines of her brightly printed cotton dress. With a little squeeze to her waist, he stopped and planted a light kiss on her forehead. "Although how you manage to stay so lovely despite the ravages of farm life, I can't imagine."

Lindsay laughed, cheered as ever by the actor's flamboyant presence.

"But I love it, Roger," she told him happily. "I've always enjoyed the feel of the land."

Roger sighed. "'She is beautiful, and therefore to be woo'd; she is woman, therefore to be won,'" he quoted, the immortal words from *King Henry VI* delivered in the full, rich resonant tones of his stage voice. "But alas, how can I win you when you insist on tilling the soil? You were meant for greater things, my dear Lindsay. Let me take you away from all this."

"Oh, and where might that be? All the way to Auckland?" said John Maclennan facetiously as he joined them. "I'm not sure that's much of an improvement, Roger." The ruddy-faced director looked particularly jovial today, and Lindsay was sure he was still riding the crest of acclaim that had greeted his latest production. *Hedda Gabler,* thanks largely to Sara Warner, had been their most successful play to date.

"Ah, but I have every intention of going on to bigger and better things, John," Roger told him confidently. "I am, as they say, merely using the Meade Theatre to pay my dues to the profession."

"Well, you'd better stick around for the next installment," the director laughed. "I'm counting on you and Sara for another sterling performance in my next production."

"And you will have it," Roger said magnanimously. He looked at Lindsay meaningfully. "I have no intention of leaving New Zealand just yet."

A few minutes after she left the director and Roger Nicolson, Lindsay spied Philip crossing the lawn escorting Sara and Matthew Warner toward the house. The actress was radiant in a sapphire-blue dress that emphasized her narrow waist and long, slender legs. Her father was dressed comfortably in brown wool slacks and a tan cashmere jacket.

"Sara, Mr. Warner," Lindsay greeted them, forcing

herself to smile with a graciousness she wished she could feel. "It's so good to see you both again."

"Yes, for a neighbor you certainly keep to yourself," said the rancher. "I don't think I've seen you once since the party."

Lindsay recoiled inwardly at the mention of that night, although she managed to retain her smile. "We've been pretty busy, Mr. Warner," she explained, certain he had heard of their difficulties. "I didn't mean to be antisocial."

"No, I'm sure you didn't," Sara said. She smiled fondly at the vintner. "I've told Philip he ought to be ashamed, working you so hard. You must be exhausted."

"I don't mind, Sara," Lindsay protested, hardly able to look at the two as they stood linked intimately arm in arm. "I've grown to love Kia Ora."

As she looked at Philip and the actress, she was once again struck by what a handsome couple they made: Philip, his black hair and cobalt eyes so brazenly masculine; Sara, with her flaming auburn hair and emerald eyes, the ultimate female. How could any man resist the magnetism, the totally feminine appeal of this woman? she asked herself hopelessly. Why had she ever allowed herself to imagine she might have a chance of winning Philip away?

Suddenly, she could no longer bear to stand there; the proximity of the lovers was just too painful.

"If you'll excuse me," she said, starting for the kitchen, "I think it's time to bring out the food."

Lunch was spectacular, thanks mainly to Inia, who had been working on the menu for the past three days. The food served at the festival was *hangi,* meaning the traditional Polynesian-style feast had been cooked in an underground pit. The *kai,* or food, included the pork and chicken from the pit, as well as marinated fish, seafood and *kumera,* or Maori sweet potato. The women had also prepared several delicious salads and large, savory loaves of warm Maori bread. And everywhere were bowls of fresh fruit and cheese as well as crackers, nuts and, of course, every possible kind of wine.

After the feast was cleared away and the wine glasses refilled, there was entertainment, a treat even more enjoyable than Lindsay expected. First came the Maori singers, who serenaded them with traditional island songs and ballads; then a spirited dance troupe performed several Maori dances including the exciting *haka,* or war dance, which was greeted by wild applause. Then, just as she thought the entertainment was finished, Lindsay was surprised to discover that the best had been saved for last.

As if prompted by an invisible sign, the drummers on the stand began a slow, rhythmic beat with a heady, South Sea Island flavor. They were soon joined by moody woodwinds and saucy maracas. As the cadence became more insistent, Kiri, in native costume, moved gracefully in front of the stand, her lithe body swaying sensuously to the jungle beat of the drums. The audience sat entranced as every muscle, every sinew of her slim body seemed to undulate in perfect rhythm to the primitive music. And Lindsay stared with the rest, almost holding her breath at the sheer beauty of the girl's movements.

Gradually, the tempo increased until, with a flurry of movement, Kiri seemed to become one with the instruments, a graceful counterpoint to their harmony. The girl seemed to fly as she twirled, her feet hardly touching the ground. Her arms, fluid expressions of supple grace, spoke with a silent, ancient language.

Then it was over, and as the girl fell fluidly to the ground, there was utter silence, followed by tremendous applause. Lindsay found she was clapping as hard as the rest, finding it hard to believe that anyone could be so graceful, so in tune with herself and her music.

"That girl is exactly what I need," an excited voice said from behind her. Lindsay turned to find John Maclennan staring enraptured at the Maori girl. "She's just the dancer we need for our next production. Who in the world is she?"

After Lindsay explained, the director insisted on an immediate introduction to the girl, during which he insisted she appear the following week at the Meade Theatre to try out for the new play. Almost beside herself with excitement, Kiri eagerly agreed.

"This is even better than being a model," she cried, hugging Lindsay in her enthusiasm. "I've always danced for fun. But I never thought anyone would pay me to do it. Wait until I tell Mama."

Lindsay was delighted with Kiri's good fortune, but her thoughts soon returned to other, more pressing matters. Now that the entertainment was over, the band had begun a kind of drumroll, which Lindsay knew announced that the big moment had arrived. It was time to open the varietals.

Smiling confidently, Philip strode to the tasting table, which was just to the right of the bandstand. All the other wines had been removed, leaving the table clear for the special opening. Since her tasting lesson with Rudy, Lindsay knew that the clean, white tablecloth, freshly changed from the one used earlier in the afternoon, was necessary so that the color of the wine might be more readily examined with the cloth as a background. Five men and one woman, who had been invited to act as official tasters, assembled around Philip. All of them, Lindsay knew, were professionals, and each had a solid reputation in the industry as impartial and skillful judges of wine. Set out before the tasters were more than a dozen tulip-shaped glasses, three dishes of crackers and bread crumbs and six spittoonlike receptacles, one next to each judge. And standing in the center of the table was the slim bottle of Cabernet Sauvignon, the first of the varietals to be officially evaluated, the small, seemingly innocent container that had the power to make or break Kia Ora within the next few minutes.

"Ladies and gentlemen," Philip began in a loud, clear voice, his manner and expression in no way betraying the inner tension he surely must be feeling. "We finally come to the crux of our celebration, the moment of truth, as they say in the bullring." He paused and waited until the amused murmurs subsided. "As most of you know," he went on, "for the past ten years Kia Ora Vineyard has had a very special and ambitious project—the development of a quality varietal that would bring pride and prestige to the Henderson Valley. We chose for our purposes a grape that has long been considered the king of red wines, a fruit that traces its origin to the great wine-producing area of Bordeaux: Cabernet Sauvignon. After considerable study"—he nodded at Richard Hansen—"it was our feeling that this grape would develop its best balance and character in our climatic zone, which is blessed with sunny days during the growing season to build the sugar in the grapes, and cool nights to maintain the level of acidity. So, the great experiment began, and now, ten years after the first Cabernet Sauvignon vines were planted, we're gathered to reap either your praise or your condemnation." He smiled at the six judges, three seated on either side of him. "Gentlemen, and Ms. Winston, are you ready?"

The six tasters nodded, then watched carefully, as

did everyone else in the garden, as Philip skillfully and quickly removed the cork from the bottle. Moving about to each taster, he poured a small amount of Cabernet Sauvignon into their glasses, about the equivalent of two small mouthfuls. There was a complete silence now in the garden, and each guest felt the tension that had settled over the long table as the drama began to unfold. Lindsay could hardly keep her eyes off Philip as she sensed the strain he was hiding so well behind those remarkable blue eyes. As soon as each taster had been served, the vintner returned to the center of the table, and Lindsay marveled that he could appear so calm when her heart was literally racing in her breast.

Now every eye in the garden was riveted on the judges as they began their critical examination of the varietal. Ten years of work, of pain and of sacrifice would now be judged by these half dozen people. Kia Ora's fate, *her* fate and Philip's, was in their hands. What if they didn't like the flavor? What if the color or bouquet did not come up to their arbitrary specifications? She had a sudden, crazy impulse to stop them, to challenge their audacity, their utter presumptuousness to stand in judgment of another man's dream.

But it was too late, the tests had begun. Holding the glass by the stem, each judge tipped it to about a forty-five-degree angle over the white tablecloth and closely studied the color. Lindsay knew from what Rudy had told her that they were noting the spectrum of tones, from the point at which the liquid made contact with the glass down to the center, or "eye," of the wine. A cheap wine, he had said, normally has only three or four distinct color tones, but a high-quality wine usually has many more.

Seemingly satisfied with the color, the judges went

on to the next test, silently twirling the wine around so that the smell was released, before taking a few short sniffs over the rim. After all six judges had performed this test, Lindsay watched nervously as two of them swirled the liquid again, repeating the sniffing process one more time before going on to the actual tasting. Was there something wrong with the aroma? she wondered, feeling a sudden, cold panic. Rudy had said much could be told about a wine simply from sniffing its bouquet. What had Philip's wine said to the judges?

And then they were lifting the glasses to their lips for the first taste. She watched them take a small quantity of wine slowly into their mouths and knew from doing it herself that they would allow it to run over the tongue before squeezing it up to the top of the palate, then under the tongue, around the gums and, finally, inside the cheeks of the bottom jaw. Only then would the wine be spit out into the waiting urns as each judge went on to the final test, the aftertaste.

Lindsay brushed a hand across her brow and was surprised to discover she was perspiring despite the coolness of the late afternoon. She tried to read some sign of encouragement in the judges' expressions, but their looks were stoic, controlled, and it was impossible to guess at their true feelings about the wine. She would have to wait, along with the rest, for the final verdict.

As the six people seated at the table prepared to evaluate the aftertaste, Lindsay noticed they seemed to breathe out through their noses immediately after spitting out the wine. She knew from Rudy's explanation that this procedure gave an impression like an echo of the taste of the wine. Then, finally, each of the judges repeated the procedure with the last mouthful remaining in the glass, only this time, instead of spitting out the wine, they swallowed it. Again, the tasters' faces were unfathomable.

The tension in the garden was unbearable as everyone waited while the judges conferred with each other, comparing notes in a whispered conference that showed no signs of haste. Lindsay knew that one question was uppermost in all their minds as they watched the judges debate: was Kia Ora's Cabernet Sauvignon worthy of the time, money and risk it had required, or was it just another red wine, no better and no worse than the rest?

Lindsay's eyes went again to Philip, and she longed to reach out to him, to touch him, to assure him that no matter what happened her love for him would never change. But she could not move; her body was so tense she could only watch as the head taster rose from his chair and turned to the crowd, his face a blank, dispassionate mask. The man was in his mid-fifties, tall, well over six feet, with a full head of salt-and-pepper hair and deep brown eyes. Under normal circumstances, Lindsay would have found him handsome, even distinguished, but this afternoon he seemed only distant and cruel, indifferent to the Herculean responsibility that had been accorded him and his colleagues. He stood for a moment looking out over the assemblage, then turned his cool eyes to the vintner. And when he did, suddenly, wonderfully, miraculously, his face broke into a wide smile.

"Congratulations, Philip," he beamed. "The verdict is unanimous. Your Cabernet Sauvignon is superb! I think you're going to put New Zealand's Henderson Valley on the map after all."

Lindsay could hardly believe her ears, and for a moment she stared at Philip in astonishment. He had done it. *They* had done it. Kia Ora's future was secure. The vineyard would not have to be sold!

Frantically, Lindsay tried to catch Philip's eye over the crowd that was moving toward the table, the heightened tension they had all felt dissipating itself now in profuse praise and congratulations. Trying to get to him herself, she squirmed forward only to find someone else had reached him first. The beautiful Sara Warner was already in his arms, her radiant face tilted up to his, their arms locked tightly around each other. A sharp pain stabbed through her heart as she watched Philip bend his head and press his lips onto hers, holding her so close in his arms that despite the noisy crowd around them they seemed lost in their own private world. When they finally broke apart they were greeted by loud cheers and hoots as the enthusiastic crowd pushed even closer.

"Wait a minute," Philip laughed, stepping up behind him onto the bandstand. He reached down and helped Sara up the stairs, then left his arm around her slim waist as he turned to face the crowd. "Make room for Sara's father." The vintner motioned to the tall rancher to join them at the top of the stand. "Let him through, everyone. I have a very special announcement to make."

The crowd gradually parted as Matthew Warner moved to stand beside his beaming daughter and the tall, handsome vintner. Then, the group was totally hushed as Philip Macek once again began to speak.

"Without Matthew and Sara Warner none of this could have been possible. They've been more than just neighbors, even more than friends. You must know that in a very real sense they are family—"

But Lindsay did not wait to know. Already she was out of the garden and making her way blindly up the stairs to her room, as far away as possible from the happy pair who stood on the bandstand about to announce their future life together as man and wife. As quickly as possible she planned to be out of the house and off the vineyard. And, for the remainder of her days, she would be out of Philip Macek's life.

10

Once again she had been forced to call on Roger, who, as usual, came readily to her rescue, no questions asked. And now, as they sped toward Auckland, all she felt was a blessed numbness, an overwhelming sense of emptiness, which, if nothing else, at least served to dull the pain. Leaving Kia Ora had been like cutting out a vital part of herself, and now only a shell remained to mourn for what might have been.

It had required only a few minutes to pack. Penning a quick, tearful goodbye to Stephanie had proved considerably more difficult. There was no doubt she would miss the child terribly; she had grown entirely too fond of her during her stay at Kia Ora. Yet there was no other recourse. She had tried her best and failed. Despite all her resolution, her determination to win, Philip had chosen to share his life with his childhood sweetheart. And suddenly the pain was even greater than her love for the vineyard. It was time to cut her losses before the hurt went any deeper. She would think about what came next later. Right now it was important only to get away, to put as much distance as possible between herself and Philip Macek.

She checked into the hotel with hardly a glance at her surroundings. Declining Roger's offer of a quiet supper, Lindsay pleaded fatigue, which was certainly true enough. Suddenly she was exhausted, not only from the frantic labors of the past six weeks but also from a far more devastating mental fatigue. Her mind felt dazed, and she wondered almost academically if she were suffering from a kind of shock.

As soon as she was settled, Roger left, but not before extracting a promise that she'd see him the next day. Lindsay agreed without much enthusiasm, realizing that until she saw Mr. Bermann, Alex's lawyer, there was little she could do to expedite her departure from New Zealand. There were papers that would have to be signed relinquishing her share of Kia Ora. Then, the operation would be complete, the growth removed and she could begin a new life, a life no longer complicated, or made more joyous, she added ruefully, by Philip Macek.

The night was interminably long. Lindsay had expected to have difficulty sleeping, but she could not have foreseen the truly physical anguish that precluded rest. Finally, after hours of fretful tossing, she got up and went to the window, looking out at the sleeping city below. Once before she had enjoyed this sight, that morning just before dawn when Philip had driven them to Mount Eden after the *Hedda Gabler* cast party. He had kissed her there, bathed in the ethereal light of a new day, and she had felt her senses explode beneath his knowing touch, found herself wanting him with a hunger she had not thought possible. Then, when she'd responded, when she had been powerless to suppress any longer the emotions she had stifled for two years, he had rejected her, had accused her of playing a game to make him sell Kia Ora. Was it because of his intense hatred for his cousin that he'd turned around and played another kind of game with her, a treacherous game that caused her to fall hopelessly in love with a man whose heart belonged to someone else? Was this what he had done to Stephanie's mother? That was another warning signal she should have heeded, she told herself bitterly. The signs had been there, she had just been too much in love to read them.

For above all else, the ultimate humiliation was that Lindsay felt used. Philip had wanted her only physically, had dallied with her to bide the time until he could formally announce his engagement to Sara. Of course he'd waited until he was certain the varietals were a success. Philip was far too proud to ask any woman to share an uncertain future. Although *she* would have, Lindsay thought dolefully. She would have faced the very devil himself with Philip Macek by her side.

Dry-eyed, Lindsay went back to bed, but not to sleep. Well, Philip had won. As of Monday he would be the sole owner of Kia Ora Vineyard, with no greenhorn partner to get in his way. He would have had his final revenge on Alex, and, she thought ruefully, on the woman who would never stop loving him.

The next day, she and Roger picnicked in Albert Park, a pleasant retreat just a few minutes walk east of her hotel on Queen Street. The day was beautiful, the sky as clear and blue as it had been for the harvest celebration the day before. But Lindsay did not want to think about yesterday, or any of the other yesterdays of her life since she'd arrived at Kia Ora. From now on she would have to put the past, and especially Philip Macek, behind her. All that mattered was the future, a future that included a one-way ticket home as soon as possible.

But despite her resolutions to forget, it seemed as if everything around her had conspired to make her remember. The picnic itself reminded her of the one she and Philip had shared just weeks ago in the beautiful Parnell Rose Gardens. And how could she forget the fateful ride to Pakatoa Island that had followed, or the storm that had linked her heart forever with his? It was no use, she sighed, looking across the park at the groups of happy picnickers. She simply could not put the vintner out of her mind, could not ease the pain which gnawed insidiously, constantly, at her heart.

"That bad, huh?" Roger said finally, and Lindsay knew he had guessed her secret. Mutely, she nodded, so close to tears she did not trust herself to speak.

He sighed, and tilted her chin toward him, studying her face closely in the bright sunlight.

"Just as I feared. There's no mistaking that hangdog expression on your lovely face. My expert diagnosis is that you are afflicted with a very severe case of unrequited love. The cure, of course, is to 'requite' it as soon as possible. And, fortunately for you, my dear Lindsay, I am dedicating myself completely to you for that purpose."

Her response to this was totally unexpected, especially to Lindsay. At the sight of Roger's sympathetic face, the tears that she had earlier held at bay flowed now with all the pent-up force of her misery. She clung to Roger as he took her into his arms, like a drowning person clutches at a lifeline. Finally, her tears spent, she drew away, embarrassed by the sudden outburst.

"Better now?" he asked, kissing her gently on the cheek. Then he ran his tongue over his mouth. "Has anyone ever told you you have very salty tears?" he teased.

"Oh, Roger," she laughed, digging through her purse in search of a tissue. "What would I do without you?"

"Exactly what I suspect you *will* do," he said softly. "I suppose you plan to go back to the States?" The question had a tentative ring, as if he was hoping for a denial.

"Yes," she said quietly, "tomorrow. As soon as I've seen the lawyer."

"And you won't change your mind?" There was no mistaking the expectant note now.

Lindsay shook her head sadly, then reached over and took his hand in hers. "I'm afraid not, Roger. Although if anyone could tempt me it would be you. I can't tell you how much I've appreciated your friendship. After, when this is over, I'll remember you were always there when I needed a friend."

That night she slept soundly, whether from sheer exhaustion or Roger's therapy in the park, she wasn't sure. But by morning she was feeling much more like her old self, in body, at least, if not in mind. The hurt was still there, but it was more like a dull ache now, an ache she suspected might never completely go away.

She called the lawyer at nine o'clock, and, although surprised at her request, Mr. Bermann agreed to see her early that afternoon. Next, she called the airport and made a reservation for an early-evening flight for the States. Only then, after all her arrangements had been made, did she permit herself to relax. Sitting back with a cup of coffee, she contemplated the results of her recent actions. In four hours she would make the final break with Philip, and, she thought dejectedly, with Kia Ora. How she would miss Stephie and Inia, and yes, Rudy, with his careworn face and twinkling Irish blue eyes. Why had she allowed herself to fall in love with all of them when she had known from the onset how hopeless it was with Philip? After her experiences with Alex, surely she should have known better. But of course she hadn't, and recriminations at this point were useless. She knew what had to be done, and the sooner it was over and behind her, the better. It was time to start a new life and forget the old.

Lindsay was in Mr. Bermann's office promptly at one o'clock. And, true to his word, the lawyer had all the necessary papers ready and waiting for her signature.

"Now, you're quite sure you want to do this, Mrs. Macek?" he asked, looking at her as if she must be out of her mind to sign away her share of the vineyard so close to the deadline date. "You realize what you're giving up?"

"Yes, Mr. Bermann," she answered, knowing only too well what she would be leaving behind. "I've given my decision a great deal of thought. I want to sign."

"But there are only two more weeks until you have satisfied the requirements of Josef Macek's will. Surely you could stay on that much longer."

Lindsay remembered Philip and Sara standing together arm-in-arm on the bandstand, ready to announce their engagement. Even now, the memory cut deep.

"No," she said decisively, "I'm afraid I couldn't stay there even two more *days.*" She rubbed at a spot between her eyes that had begun to throb painfully. "Can I see the papers now, Mr. Bermann? I really would like to get this over with."

The lawyer looked at her over his reading glasses, his long thin face creased with concern, and she could see slight beads of perspiration on his nearly bald pate.

"Well, er, unfortunately, Mrs. Macek, there are one or two unforeseen difficulties," he told her nervously. "You see, the papers—"

"—require my signature as well," came the all-too-familiar voice that she had thought she would never hear again.

Spinning around, her heart pounding erratically in her breast, Lindsay saw Philip standing just inside the doorway, his dark blue eyes fixed rigidly on her.

"Philip!" she cried, half getting up from her chair. "But I didn't expect—"

"To see me again?" he finished for her. "No, I don't suppose you did. But you neglected to read my uncle's will in its entirety," he went on, the biting edge of his low voice cutting through her like a knife. "It clearly states that *both* partners' signatures are required if one of them decides to renounce their share of the property."

"But how did you know I'd be here?"

"A mutual friend told me," he answered elusively. "A friend who seems to feel you're making a mistake."

Roger, Lindsay thought suddenly. The "friend" must be Roger. Although why he would tell Philip her plans, she couldn't imagine. Nonetheless, Philip's presence mustn't deter her, mustn't make her lose control. If anything, his being here could expedite matters. Now she wouldn't have to wait until he had signed the papers to catch her plane.

"Why did you leave like that, Lindsay?" he asked before she could speak.

She had not expected to have to answer that question, especially not in person. She had not anticipated having to look again into those penetrating eyes. They threatened to draw her into perilous depths of emotions she had vowed never to succumb to again. He must not guess the real reason she had left, how very successful his plan had been, how deeply he had hurt her. Lifting her chin, Lindsay gathered her wounded pride around her like a shield.

"I'm surprised you couldn't guess," she said indifferently. "You always said I would find Kia Ora boring and, well, frankly, I did." She gestured wearily with her hand. "Oh, it was exciting enough when there was a chance we might lose the crop. But after that—well, it really did get rather tiresome. I think it's time I got back to my real friends." She looked directly into his eyes, unable to resist one parting thrust. "Besides, I'm sure one Mrs. Macek is quite sufficient for any household."

He looked confused. "*One* Mrs. Macek?"

Lindsay was losing patience. Why was he tormenting her like this? What game was he playing now? "Your wife," she said pointedly. "Sara."

But Philip still didn't seem to comprehend. "Sara? But surely you don't think—?" He stopped and looked from Lindsay to the lawyer, who sat staring at the two of them equally bewildered. Then, suddenly, inexplicably, Philip laughed, a full, robust sound which echoed through the musty room. "But that's wonderful," he boomed, and he reached across the large oak desk to wring the lawyer's hand in a vigorous handshake. "That explains everything."

In one long stride, Philip was at Lindsay's chair, and with both arms he literally lifted her out of her seat.

"Philip—what in the world—?"

"You're coming with me, Lindsay," he told her with a determination that brooked no argument. "It seems our mutual friend was right, after all. You were about to make one hell of a big mistake. And, by God, so was I!"

"But why didn't you tell me?" Lindsay asked again, still unable to comprehend that Philip was here, next to her, looking at her as if nothing had happened to pull them apart. They were sitting on a bench in a small park off Quay Street, only blocks from where they'd picnicked in Parnell Gardens on the day she'd first discovered she loved him. Maybe she was just dizzy from the events of the past hour, but she had the feeling the wheel had come full circle, that she was back again at the beginning.

"I didn't tell you because you never asked," he answered, smiling reasonably. He sat holding her hand possessively, as if he were afraid she might break away and run from him again if he let go. "And it never occurred to me you might think Sara and I were planning an engagement."

"But John Maclennan—Kiri—the whole cast of the play—everyone expected you to announce your engagement at the harvest celebration."

"And you listened to them." Philip shook his head until an unruly lock of black hair fell over one eye, giving him a tousled, roguish look. "And worse, you believed what they said. Haven't you ever heard of gossip, my dear Hollywood innocent? I would think

180

you'd be more than used to it, coming from the gossip capital of the world."

"I wasn't emotionally involved with the movie stars," she laughed. "Besides, every time you looked at her it seemed so obvious. And then, that night in the garden—"

"I had just clinched a deal with her father that assured us we would get through the harvest. And Sara had done a bang-up job of going to bat for me." At her disbelieving look he went on, "That's why I wanted to talk to Matthew privately the night of his party—to ask for a loan."

"But why didn't you tell me?" Lindsay asked, sick that so much heartache could have been so easily avoided.

"I didn't tell you about the loan because I didn't want you to worry. You were already working much harder than I expected. In fact, you surprised the hell out of me. Here I'd imagined Alex's widow to be his carbon copy, a soft, pampered Hollywood jet-setter. Instead I found myself with another field hand. And a damn good one at that."

Lindsay looked at him sheepishly. "I guess I have to take some of the blame for that impression," she told him diffidently. "I was too proud to tell you that Alex and I separated two years ago. We were worlds apart, had been from the beginning, only I'd been too blind to recognize the signs. Finally, I couldn't take his infidelities any longer and I left. At the time of his death I hadn't seen him in two years." She looked at him dubiously. "But all this still doesn't explain the announcement at the celebration yesterday. I was sure you were going to tell everyone of your engagement to Sara."

"And you didn't bother to stay to hear what I really had to say." Philip stroked her cheek gently with the back of his hand. "Darling, I wanted it to be a surprise. If the Cabernet Sauvignon had failed, then, of course, I would have said nothing. But I felt it only fitting that the first varietals be dedicated to Matthew Warner."

There was so much to comprehend. Lindsay felt decidedly muddled as she tried to make some sense of the puzzle.

"But I still don't understand the scene in the Warners' garden the night of his party," she said, trying to sort out that little matter once and for all. "You seemed so—so *friendly*."

Philip lowered his eyes and rubbed her fingers gently as he tried to explain. "The gossip you heard was right in some respects," he admitted slowly. "Sara and I have known each other since she was a little girl. Of course I was ten years older than Sara, but it was natural enough when our friends assumed later on we might get married. Yet as much as I care for Sara, I guess I always knew that marriage with her would never be right. Our lives are too different. I found myself continually finding excuses not to set a date."

He took her other hand into his and looked intently into her face as if trying to read her reaction. "That night in the garden, I was fresh from discovering what real love was all about, Lindsay. Once I had found you, it was clear, and suddenly I couldn't find a single excuse for not settling down. In fact, I couldn't wait." He gave her hands a little squeeze. "That was a congratulatory kiss you saw, darling. I had just told Sara the good news about us. I think she understands. Our worlds are too far apart for us to have made a go of it."

Lindsay's cheeks flushed as she realized how foolish she had been, how deeply she must have hurt Philip that night she had had Roger take her home from the party. Still, there were unanswered questions. This was the time to clear the air.

"But you and Sara were upstairs, alone, in your room. I saw you coming down the day she visited Kia Ora."

"Of course," he said simply. "I was showing her my etchings."

"Your what?" For a moment Lindsay could think of nothing but the old gag, the time-worn line used to lure a young woman into a man's lair. At her expression, Philip laughed out loud, causing amused glances from several adjoining benches.

"My etchings. *Literally*, I mean. Didn't you notice them the night you were up in my room?"

Suddenly Lindsay remembered the exquisite gold etchings she had admired hanging in Philip's bedroom. But so much had happened that day, that night; it was no wonder she'd forgotten them.

"I had just bought them the week before you arrived," he went on, still amused by her startled expression. "Lindsay, Sara and I have known each other for most of our lives. It was only natural I should want to share something new with her."

Catching her breath, Lindsay leaned back against the park bench. His explanations were spinning her world, throwing everything she had believed topsy-turvy. It would take some time for it to sink in, for her to readjust her thinking. But there was one last doubt, one unresolved issue, and it was the most difficult of all to broach.

"Philip," she started hesitantly, "what happened with Stephanie's mother?"

When he went pale beneath his deep tan, she almost wished she had let the past lie undisturbed. What had happened all those years ago surely should be beyond her concern now. Yet, she could not let go of this final question. She had to know the truth. There could be no more doubts, even about the past.

"Only three people know what I'm about to tell you, Lindsay," he said soberly, "and two of them are dead. It must never be mentioned again, not even between the two of us. Is that agreed?"

Lindsay looked into Philip's eyes before she answered. Never had she seen them so earnest, so intense. Slowly, not taking her eyes off his, she nodded her acceptance of his conditions.

"Stephanie is not my daughter," he told her, so softly that she had to lean closer to hear. "Ten years ago I was engaged to marry a beautiful girl. She was very young, barely nineteen, and extremely naive. I was twenty-seven and just coming into my own on the vineyard. I felt very sure of myself, very certain of my future and of my place in the world of viniculture. And at the time of my engagement I was very sure of our love for each other. I was on top of the world. It was a good time to be alive."

A shadow crossed Philip's handsome face and Lindsay had to resist the impulse to reach out and soothe away the hurt. But she could sense what this admission was costing him, even now, ten years later. She must let him finish his tale uninterrupted. In a moment he went on.

"The one factor I had not counted on in my little cocoon of happiness was my dear cousin, gallant Alex, who could never keep his hands off a pretty girl, even one who belonged to someone else."

Lindsay gasped. "You mean that Alex—?"

Philip nodded. "Alex is Stephanie's father. As soon as I found out I confronted him, made him promise to marry the girl. And I must say he was amicable enough about it. Rather than fight me he gave in, said he'd ask her the next day." Philip's look was frightening as he remembered that tragic day so long ago. "But all he did the next day was to leave Kia Ora forever, breaking the girl's heart and his own father's in the bargain. Neither of them ever really got over it. When Stephie was barely six months old her mother simply couldn't stand it any longer. The shame of her pregnancy and losing Alex like that were more than she could bear. So one day—"

This time she did reach out to take his hands. "I know," she said softly. "Kiri told me. She took her life. And you took Stephanie to raise as your own."

"I loved her, as if she were my own, even from the beginning. She was a beautiful baby. Any man would have been proud to claim paternity."

"Except Alex," Lindsay said, feeling a deep sense of shame for the man who had been her husband. No wonder Philip still held his cousin in such contempt, still reviled his memory ten years later. It wasn't just the hurt Alex had caused *him*, although that must have been considerable; it was what he had done to a young, vulnerable girl and an old man. And, perhaps worst of all, the legacy he had bequeathed to an innocent child.

"So, when you came here to claim Alex's inheritance," he went on, "I'm afraid I wasn't ready to greet you with open arms. I had no reason to believe you'd be any different than he'd been. For a while I even thought that, through you, Alex had come back from the grave to take whatever he could from the land."

Lindsay was silent for a moment, absorbing the enormity of what Philip had just told her. When she turned back to him, her eyes were brimming with love for this man who had suffered so much.

"It seems only right, then, that Alex's widow should

come back to be mother to the little girl he deserted, doesn't it?" Then, she added softly, "That is, if her father wants me."

Lindsay's heart nearly burst from the love she saw in Philip's face as he took her into his arms.

"Want you?" he whispered. "Let me show you how much her father wants you, my darling."

Philip cupped her chin in his hand; then, tilting her face upward, he brought his lips to hers, kissing her with a hunger that both of them knew would take the rest of their lives to satisfy. Joyfully surrendering to his embrace, Lindsay locked her arms around his neck, eager, at last, to reap the bountiful fruit from their own special harvest of love.

Silhouette Desire
15-Day Trial Offer

A new romance series that explores contemporary relationships in exciting detail

Six Silhouette Desire romances, free for 15 days!
We'll send you six new Silhouette Desire romances to look over for 15 days, absolutely free! If you decide not to keep the books, return them and owe nothing.

Six books a month, free home delivery. If you like Silhouette Desire romances as much as we think you will, keep them and return your payment with the invoice. Then we will send you six new books every month to preview, just as soon as they are published. You pay only for the books you decide to keep, and you never pay postage and handling.

 — — MAIL TODAY — — — —

Silhouette Desire, Dept. SDSDJH
120 Brighton Road, Clifton, NJ 07012

Please send me 6 Silhouette Desire romances to keep for 15 days, absolutely free. I understand I am not obligated to join the Silhouette Desire Book Club unless I decide to keep them.

Name_____

Address_____

City_____

State_____ Zip_____

This offer expires April 30, 1983

Silhouette Desire

Coming Next Month

Lover In Pursuit by Stephanie James

Reyna McKenzie vowed she'd never again succumb to Trevor Langdon's promise of love. But he'd come to Hawaii determined to reclaim her and under the tropical sun, she soon found herself willing to submit to the love she so desperately wanted.

King Of Diamonds by Penny Allison

Carney Gallagher was baseball's golden boy, now in his troubled last season. Flame-haired Jo Ryan, the Atlanta *Star*'s rookie woman sports reporter, made her first career hit at his expense. Gallagher vowed to even the score . . . but Jo never imagined that passion would be the weapon of his choice.

Love In The China Sea by Judith Baker

Kai Shanpei, mysterious Eurasian tycoon, was as much a part of Hong Kong as its crescent harbor, teeming streets and the jagged mountains looming above. From the moment she met him Anne Hunter was lost in his spell, plucked from reality and transported into his arms to learn the secrets of love.

Silhouette Desire

Coming Next Month

Bittersweet In Bern by Cheryl Durant

Gabi Studer couldn't resist Peter Imhof's offer of work in Switzerland, but she hadn't reckoned on living in the same magnificent Alpine chalet as the famed author. Alone together on the enchanted Swiss mountainside, temptation was only a kiss away.

Constant Stranger by Linda Sunshine

Murphy Roarke literally knocked Joanna Davenport off her feet. She'd come to New York to launch a publishing career, and Roarke had helped her every step of the way . . . until he stole her heart, demanding that she choose between the job of a lifetime and a stormy, perilous love.

Shared Moments by Mary Lynn Baxter

He was the devil in disguise. Kace McCord, the silver-haired client Courtney Roberts tried to keep at arm's length. But he took possession of her from the first, arousing her feelings and driving her to heights of rapture.

YOU'LL BE SWEPT AWAY
WITH SILHOUETTE DESIRE

$1.75 each

1 ☐ CORPORATE AFFAIR
Stephanie James

2 ☐ LOVE'S SILVER WEB
Nicole Monet

3 ☐ WISE FOLLY
Rita Clay

4 ☐ KISS AND TELL
Suzanne Carey

5 ☐ WHEN LAST WE LOVED
Judith Baker

6 ☐ A FRENCHMAN'S KISS
Kathryn Mallory

7 ☐ NOT EVEN FOR LOVE
Erin St. Claire

8 ☐ MAKE NO PROMISES
Sherry Dee

9 ☐ MOMENT IN TIME
Suzanne Simms

10 ☐ WHENEVER I LOVE YOU
Alana Smith

$1.95 each

11 ☐ VELVET TOUCH
Stephanie James

12 ☐ THE COWBOY AND THE
LADY Diana Palmer

13 ☐ COME BACK, MY LOVE
Pamela Wallace

14 ☐ BLANKET OF STARS
Lorraine Valley

15 ☐ SWEET BONDAGE
Dorothy Vernon

16 ☐ DREAM COME TRUE
Ann Major

17 ☐ OF PASSION BORN
Suzanne Simms

18 ☐ SECOND HARVEST
Erin Ross

SILHOUETTE DESIRE, Department SD/6
1230 Avenue of the Americas
New York, NY 10020

Please send me the books I have checked above. I am enclosing $_____
(please add 50¢ to cover postage and handling. NYS and NYC residents
please add appropriate sales tax). Send check or money order—no cash or
C.O.D.'s please. Allow six weeks for delivery.

NAME _____

ADDRESS _____

CITY _____ STATE/ZIP _____

Silhouette Desire

Now Available

Sweet Bondage by Dorothy Vernon

Maxwell Ross had set into motion a plan to avenge his younger brother. But he was wreaking revenge on the wrong woman, as Gemma Coleridge was only too happy to tell him—at first. But soon, too soon, her heart overrode her head. She lost her anger in Maxwell's arms, and dared to dream of a happiness that would last forever.

Dream Come True by Ann Major

Six years after their divorce, Barron Skymaster, superstar, tried to claim Amber again. But how could she face him after denying him knowledge of his own son—a son he had every right to know? Would that knowledge bring them together again or would it tear them apart forever?

Of Passion Born by Suzanne Simms

Professor Chelsie McBride was thoroughly acquainted with her subject—the sometimes humorous, sometimes bawdy Canterbury Tales. A respected professional in her field, she was no stranger to the earthy side of passion. But when it was introduced to her in the person of Drew Bradford, she realized she'd only been studying love by the book.

Second Harvest by Erin Ross

The fields of Kia Ora were all that remained of Alex's turbulent past, and Lindsay was bound to honor her husband's memory by taking an active part in the New Zealand vineyard. But what she began with reluctance soon became a fervent obsession. The exotic splendor of Kia Ora was captivating, and Philip Macek, its hard-driving owner, held her spellbound.

Enjoy your own special time with Silhouette Romances.

Send for 6 books today— one is yours free!

Silhouette Romances take you into a special world of thrilling drama, tender passion, and romantic love. These are enthralling stories from your favorite romance authors—tales of fascinating men and women, set in exotic locations all over the world.

Convenient free home delivery. We'll send you six exciting Silhouette Romances to look over for 15 days. If you enjoy them as much as we think you will, pay the invoice enclosed with your trial shipment. **One book is yours free to keep.** Silhouette Romances are delivered right to your door with never a charge for postage or handling. There's no minimum number of books to buy, and you may cancel at any time.

Silhouette Romances